CHASING THE RAIN

Chasing the Rain

This is a work of fiction. Names, characters, places, and incidents either are the product of the author's imagination or are used fictitiously. Any resemblance to actual animals, living or dead, events, or locales is entirely coincidental.

All rights reserved. No part of this publication may be reproduced, distributed, or transmitted in any form without the prior written permission of the publisher, except in the case of brief quotations embodied in critical reviews and certain other non-commercial uses permitted by copyright law.

Copyright © 2019 by James E. Rugman

For permissions please contact:

james.rugman@yahoo.com

Front cover design by James E. Rugman/istock.

Front cover copyright © 2019 by James E. Rugman

First printing edition 2019.

ISBN: 978-1-7974-1568-0

For Emily

CHASING THE RAIN

JAMES E. RUGMAN

1

Chasing the Rain

The pre-dawn glow peered ominously over the horizon, beneath the dark, star-speckled shadow of a twilight sky. The distant mountains looked menacing against the pale band of light at the edge of the earth. Although the rest of the savannah was yet to stir from its silent slumber, the adults among our herd had been awake for hours, nervously watching the horizon and awaiting the dreaded message that our epic journey was about to begin. The leaders had already had several meetings, but just when it seemed they'd finished, they went back to talk about something new. As the youngsters started to wake up from their blissful sleep, the parents encouraged them to feed; trying to make out the day was just like any other; it was lucky they were all too innocent to notice the anguish in their mothers' eyes.

Through the sweet smelling mist that blanketed the plain, my father kicked up clumps of dirt as he made his way back from what was hopefully the last leaders' meeting before breakfast. When the suns yellow crest finally broke its cover, the savannah was draped in a warm golden glow and the air filled with the rapturous song of the bird's morning chorus. The dew on our coats rose slowly like a veil, to reveal the vast herd of wildebeest stood steaming in the hazy dawn light of the Serengeti.

My siblings were wide awake, and as they were far too young to understand how important the day was, they were chasing each other around, laughing and screaming joyfully. Father snapped at them and they came to a skidding halt in the dust. They both looked at each other with terror on their faces, but when father's attention was drawn back to the horizon, they soon started giggling again.

My mother was really quiet, she was obviously anxious about the day ahead, especially with two new youngsters to keep an eye on. She thought she could hide her worries from all of us, but I can always tell when something's troubling her. The stress of the move was taking its toll on everyone, but it was something we had to do if we were all to survive. My parents have done this many times before, and I've done it twice myself, but I was too young to really know why, or even what was happening. Now I was old enough to see the effect it had on the rest of the herd, I could truly relate to my brother and sister, and just wish I was innocently oblivious to the whole thing too.

My breakfast was a real struggle; every mouthful of the sparse pasture was even drier than the last, but I knew I needed to eat something before we left. Father shouted at Imari again to be quiet. He told him and Karamu to fill their stomachs for the journey ahead as there's no guarantee they'll get another chance to feed before sunset. It was the first time they'd ever seen father like that and the fright made Karamu cry, so mother went over and told them both to feed; reassuring them that he didn't really mean what he said. They had only just started to walk, so this was going to be the biggest challenge they have ever had to face.

The last of the dew had long burnt off, and every detail of the savannah became clear and vibrant as the sun shone over the mountains from a cloudless azure sky. And as it rose ever higher, so did the temperature, waking all the insects that appeared as if from nowhere. The buzzing of flies would usually irritate me, but I was finding the sound oddly calming; it brought back comforting memories of the time we'd spent with loved ones on these plains the past few months. Thoughts of how safe we felt relaxing in the midday sun came flooding in with every buzz. And the elders' amazing stories that were told to the freshest of faces among the herd resonated through my heart with the rhythmic song of the cicada. But with the time for us to leave fast approaching, those memories were becoming distant dreams; ones we all hoped we'd get to see again one day.

Father gathered us all together, but without a single sound he stepped away and we watched in anticipation as he met with his closest friend Jelani. There was a deep rumble of thunder to the west, just beyond the horizon, and they both looked up expectantly before gesturing to each other that it was time for the herd to head out. Father looked back and we instantly knew to follow him, but after only a couple of steps, we were already missing the sanctity of those sacred plains we were leaving behind.

My brother and sister were being silly again so mother threw them a look which told them to stop immediately. They fell into line and continued on sensibly, letting out the occasional stifled giggle through the deafening silence. Jelani had gathered his family and they were approaching us at the same muted pace. It was clear this was making everyone wary, but we had no choice but to begin our expedition.

The open plains were hot and dusty, the sun burning brightly ahead of us as it tried desperately to dissuade us before our journey had really started. But we all pushed on with true defiance, both of the sun itself, and of our aching hearts. Father always says it's better to keep looking forward on these journeys, or you'll want to return to the place you felt most comfortable if you look back. As we pressed on with our journey, more families came together and they all looked as worried as we did. They too were already pining for the lands we all called our home, and they were all clearly fighting the same urge to turn back around.

By the time we reached the edge of our territory, the group had amassed to what must be thousands; it was hard to tell exactly how many had rejoined, but it was just a fraction that will finally make up this entire herd. This can sometimes be a hindrance as much as a blessing, as the added safety is reassuring, but there's always the risk of mass panic when the tension is high.

I gave my parents a break by looking after my siblings. They were falling behind and kept asking if we could stop, so I tried my best to keep them moving with the promise of a game of Ampe when reached our first rest stop. But this still didn't stop them complaining.

A message soon came through the crowd that we were arriving at our first important rest stop. It is an area the wildebeest know to aim for at the first signs of the storms. Here the leaders will read the pasture, and if the signs are good, then we will head to our mwanzo. This is where all our friends know to meet us, and marks the true beginning of our epic journey. This was a tense time for the leaders, but for the rest of us it would offer a welcome chance to rest and maybe even refuel. I told my siblings the news and the thought of stopping finally cheered them up.

At the rendezvous, the herd had a chance to get a drink and have the smallest bit of food to keep us going. We took the opportunity to rest and give our legs a much needed break. My parents didn't even mind that my brother Imari was chasing his sister around again; the journey is an adventure to them both, and when they play it helps them enjoy it. When Imari popped out through the herd, I joked that he couldn't be as tired as he told me he was. I could see him struggling to come up with an answer but just as he was going to speak, Karamu appeared from between my mother and Mbali. She nudged him and shouted *'you're it,'* and he turned away and chased her back through the herd with glee.

Father was speaking with Jelani as they headed over to meet the other leaders to discuss matters they'd gone over so many times before. The meetings allow them all to focus and keep from making costly mistakes. I heard Jelani say 'although this group is large Imamu, it is with you and your family that I always feel safest.' Father has always been respected within the troop, and individuals turned to him for words of support long before he was a leader, even Idriis, one of the highest elders in our herd. Father's name means "the spiritual leader" and I think this gives everyone hope. He doesn't try to stand out; he just has a naturally strong manner which lets everyone, including us, feel safe whenever we're with him.

While mother fed my siblings, she spoke with Jelani's wife, Mbali, and it was clear they were both trying to distract each other with casual conversation. Ayana, their daughter, came over to graze with me. We have known each other our whole lives and have always been really close, but I'd found it hard to even speak to her all day.

'My father is finding this morning very difficult, but Imamu is doing a good job at staying calm Berko,' she said, trying to break the awkwardness between us.

'On the outside yes,' I said quietly.

'What do you mean?'

'It's just...' I paused, 'he's really stressed, but he has a good way of hiding things for the sake of the herd. He's been snapping at my siblings and me these past few days. I worry such a burden could be too much for him to carry alone.' Ayana looked down solemnly and I knew I'd worried her too, so I tried my best to back track. 'Of course this is my father, *The Great Imamu*, the best leader this herd has ever known.' I mimicked him joyfully, pushing out my chest and standing as tall as I could. Ayana laughed at me and gave me a playful nudge. 'I know he's strong Ayana, and I know he'll lead the herd to safety. He has so many times before. But the council rely on him so heavily to take charge. There are already over a million others here, and far more are joining us by the minute. It's a massive responsibility. Even for him.'

'I guess I never really thought of it like that. Although the herd have so much respect for your father, they expect so much of him, but we never actually stop and think about Imamu. I am so sorry Berko; you must think the herd are selfish.'

'You know my father never chose to lead this march. And he doesn't dictate the route or the schedule either. This is a journey we've taken for millennia. He knows the herd need a strong leader,' I sat down in the grass and Ayana sat down beside me. 'My father has a natural ability to create calm and encourage others whenever they're struggling. When they're around him, they can feel his energy. And he knows that, so he lets them use him as their pillar of strength.'

Ayana touched her cheek to mine, a symbol of support, but it was almost like she was trying to apologise for the rest of the herd.

'Father always tells me "your life is not written, the stars will choose your fate. They are always watching and guiding you through this life, and they lead the herd to follow the brightest spirit among us." My father never chose to be a leader. But he believed the stars must have chosen him for a reason, so it's not up to him to back away from his fate.'

A murmur came through the group; it was time for us to move on. Ayana went back to her family without speaking; the thought of moving forward had made her nervous again and my words had done little to help calm her worries. By now the herd of wildebeest was at its full mass with all of the droves finally joining up as one.

Macaria and Bushira, two of our seekers, were sent back to the north of the sacred birthing grounds. Many of the wildebeest have learned to read the storms on the savannah which tell us when to move on to the next suitable grazing pasture. Our sense of smell is far greater than that of the other animals in the Serengeti, so the zebra, eland and gazelle rely on us to usher in the beginning of the epic journey. Macaria and Bushira can fly back and signal to everyone that it's time to leave. This will also attract many of our other friends who too will join our march to chase the rain.

Once the seekers were out of sight, the leaders looked one last time over the herd. They gave the signal for us all to move out, before disappearing behind the shroud of dust hanging heavily over the scorching plain.

Our anxiety was easing as we passed the foot of Lemakarot. This is the place we are most likely to be ambushed, but we saw few of our enemies in the valley. My father said quietly 'this is a promising sign that the stars are on our side,' but he was still scanning the area carefully as he spoke.

Macaria swooped in and let the leaders know our other friends had now started to join us. When I heard him say this, I was really excited. As the herd were splitting to avoid a large rocky outcrop, I headed right for it and climbed onto the highest boulder to see them all for myself. It was incredible. There were wildebeest marching as far as the eye could see. And now, just as Macaria had said, all the others were among us too. Small gazelle were leaping, appearing and vanishing out of the herd like fish breaking the rivers surface. Large groups of zebra were merging in and spreading among the wildebeest as they greeted old friends. Eland joined in the march at the same steady pace and ignored the burning heat of the sun on their backs. Giraffe proudly looked right over the herd, and when one of them saw me he lowered his head to greet me. There were rhinos trundling along, trying their best to keep up with the rest of the herd, and in the distance were some of our dear friends the elephants, marching in line on the horizon and trumpeting their joy to be among us once again. A sea of bodies stretched right to the horizon, floating above the savannah on golden clouds of dust. I felt excited for the first time on this journey. To know these animals had all come to join us meant so much, and it really showed how much my father is revered.

In my excitement I'd lost sight of my family. I needed to catch up with them quickly, so I scanned the nearest gap in the crowd and leapt down to the earth with a thud, sending a cloud of dry dirt high into the air. I forced my way through the mass of bodies, apologising all the time, until I reached my siblings walking with mother. Out of breath but too excited to care, I leant down between them and whispered through heavy gasps, 'I've just seen all our friends from the north; they've all come to join us on our march.' They both got really excited. Now they'll finally meet all the animals they've already heard so much about, and be able to put faces to the stories we've all held so dear. When I told father I'd seen the others joining the group, he smiled and looked far more relaxed. It clearly meant a lot to him to have the trust of so many.

My brother and sister were much calmer when I told them the others had joined us. They even started behaving and listening to mother when she spoke to them. My mother has been very protective over the two of them since they were born just over a month ago. Imari acts silly with Karamu, but he's actually very caring towards her. Soon after he was born, when he was still getting used to his legs, he seemed drawn towards Karamu, like she needed him more than anything else on this earth.

Karamu isn't our sister by blood; she's the daughter of my mother's half sister Nakato. But the love we all have for her bonds us just as strongly. Grandmother helped her close friend in her time of need and took Nakato on, bringing her and mother up as twins. They had a strong bond and were inseparable throughout their lives. They always stuck together and helped each other on these difficult journeys. They were even blessed with having their children at the same time this season, mothers second but Nakato's first.

As they stood together to give birth, helping each other through the process, Nakato turned to my mother and touched her cheek before whispering something in her ear. My mother gave birth to Imari who was healthy and strong, and whilst she was cleaning him in the sunlight, Nakato entered the final stages of labour. But it was apparent there was something wrong. The labour went on much longer than it should have, and Nakato became weak and had to lie down in the grass. The older females tried their best to reassure her, but she was exhausted and had no more strength to carry on. They all helped her to calf, taking hold of Karamu and aiding her arrival. One of the matriarchs was trying to keep Nakato's focus on her new daughter, but as Karamu entered into the world and took her first breath, Nakato took her last and her soul rose up to sit among the stars.

Mother was completely distraught, but she quickly stepped in to fulfil the promise she'd just made to her sister, and as she began to clean Karamu, Imari got to his feet and steadily made his way over to them both. He should have instinctively started feeding, but instead he aided his new sister, guiding her to my mother and sacrificing his first meal so she could become healthy and strong. My mother has always told me that it was at that point she saw a spark between them, and their bond was forged for an eternity.

Father and I entered the sacred birthing grounds to meet my new brother, and mother introduced us all. 'Imamu, say hello to your son.'

'He's beautiful my love... and I see he isn't alone.'

'This is Karamu, our new daughter.'

Father bent down and gave mother a loving kiss on the cheek and she told him of her sadness for Nakato. 'Karamu, a precious gift, I couldn't think of a more fitting name,' he said, and bent down to greet his two new arrivals. 'You are true gifts from the stars, both of you.' He turned again to look at mother. 'I am so proud of you Amara; you have such a strong and caring heart.'

Mother told my father how my brother had showed such devotion towards Karamu when he first saw her, and father looked at him lovingly.

He turned back towards mother and said 'such loyalty from a young age. What about the name Imari? I feel it suits him perfectly.'

'It's wonderful. Our faithful Imari,' she touched her cheek against his and he seemed to like his new name. 'Come Berko, say hello to your new siblings.'

I bent down to meet them and they both pressed their cheeks against mine. I originally felt a little worried about having a new baby brother or sister, but as soon as I met them, I was overcome with pride.

The sun was turning the entire sky a vibrant orange as we reached our mwanzo. Despite us having walked almost non-stop all day, this area has marked the true starting point for this journey since the beginning of our ancestors memories. This place lets us all feel safe because although there is little food for any of us, this means there are less places for our enemies to hide. It's within this place that everyone converges for the first time and we finally get to talk with old friends and share stories. And it's here that we get to see the true meaning of family.

While most of the herd get to rest our weary legs, the leaders of every troop meet up for the first time to discuss the coming months. They keep it relaxed and from the outside it looks like a normal social gathering, but in truth they're discussing the harsh reality of the journey we are all about to embark on. They go over the dangers and discuss the warnings and the messages they need to pass promptly throughout the group. They talk about the previous years and how they can learn from past mistakes. And then they go back over the route, even though this has barely changed for millennia. They are meticulous in every detail and are careful not to miss anything out.

My father is highly respected by the entire group, even by those from the other troops. But as I watch them now, I'm reminded of the conversation I had with

Ayana this morning. The group rely heavily on him. And although he's a strong leader, maybe the best this herd has ever seen, how can someone bear that much weight? He's been snappier recently, getting stressed with me and my siblings over the smallest things. And as I look at him now, as he speaks so passionately and shows such strength the others rely on, he seems a little distant.

2
Our Journey Begins

I woke to a murmur of excitement among the group, and as I opened my eyes I recoiled in discomfort as the bright light of the rising sun flooded in. Karamu and Imari bounded over excitedly, nudging me to get up. 'Berko, Berko mummy said we're going soon. Everyone's saying there's heavy storms over there,' said Imari excitedly, pointing to the horizon with is tiny hoof.

'Why is everyone so happy Berko?' asked Karamu, still nudging me.

'Because the rain brings life Karamu,' I yawned, still squinting through the sting of the morning light as I tried to focus on her face. 'Without it, we wouldn't have the food to keep us all going. If the storms are heavy, the grass will be lush and plentiful. They're all excited because we should get a big feast when we reach the woodlands.'

They both looked at each other and their eyes widened with excitement. They smiled widely and then skipped away happily, laughing and shouting 'we're going to eat til we pop.'

When I got up and walked over to my family, mother was talking quietly to father. Spotting me, their conversation stopped abruptly. She encouraged me to try to eat as much food as I could in case we didn't get to eat again for a while. She kissed fathers cheek and gave him a loving look as she went off to find my siblings.

Father smiled at me, 'good morning my son, did you sleep well?'

'Yes thanks. Did your meeting go well last night?'

'It did. We were able to make some good plans and our journey seems it will be a positive one this time.'

'I heard there are heavy storms to the west, everyone's really excited.'

He sighed heavily. 'It's true. But I am troubled the news has reached so far so quickly. I was hoping to keep it quiet for now.'

'Aren't you excited about the rains father?'

'Of course I am Berko,' he smiled, though his eyes were glazed and he was looking almost through me, 'the rains are important for us all.' He came over to me and spoke softly, finally looking me in the eyes. 'But they also bring danger. And even death. Everyone is so excited at the prospect of having a feast when we reach the woodlands, but the thought of a full stomach is clouding their minds. They have lost focus on what lies ahead of us. Our route is cut off by rivers and lakes. And with the heavier storms, these will be far more dangerous for us. The rivers will be powerful and the lakes could be much wider than before. This could prove difficult for all of us; it could affect the entire journey,' he glazed over again. 'And I worry the herd will lose faith in me if I steer them wrong Berko.'

Hearing my father speak like this worried me, he is usually so strong. 'You never chose this role father; the stars chose you because the herd needs someone strong to lead them. They all admire you, and you've guided them to safety too many times for them to forget this. Or to lose trust in your leadership. I know I'm your son, but there's nobody else I'd rather follow across the savannah than you.'

'Thank you Berko,' he smiled and touched his cheek to mine. 'You have shown real maturity these past few weeks, I am truly proud to be your father. Go and find your siblings, tell them we are leaving very soon.' As he turned away from me his smile disappeared and that glazed look returned to his face. He just stared into the distance like he has so many times recently. I'd hoped my words would help, but maybe I've just added more weight to his already heavily burdened shoulders.

I found the rest of my family, mother was talking with Mbali and Jelani, and Ayana was keeping my siblings entertained. I stood back, just watching the three of them playing Ampe and I felt real admiration for Ayana. She knows how stressful this journey is and how it's affecting both our families, but she's still able to stay strong for my brother and sister.

My brother won and made sure they both knew it, prancing around, boasting. 'Hey you two, I think Berko wants to play,' said Ayana as she spotted me. 'Come on then Berko; see if you can beat Imari.'

'I... I was just coming to tell you all that the herd is moving on soon. We should all make sure we've eaten something and had enough water for the journey.'

'Yes Dad!' said Ayana sarcastically. 'OK you two go and find your mother and tell her it's nearly time to go. And Karamu? Make sure Imari's head doesn't get any bigger, or it will be too heavy for him to carry on the journey.' Imari screwed up his face at Ayana and then chased after Karamu through the herd. 'So, when did you become such a spoil sport?' she said to me.

'Sorry?' I snapped. I was trying to see if my father was coming back.

'Is everything alright Berko?'

'*Ayana, come and have something to eat,*' called Mbali from the edge of the herd.

'I will catch up with you in a minute Berko, OK?' she nudged me to get my attention. 'OK Berko?'

'Sorry? Yes... I will see you soon Ayana.' I turned back to where I'd last seen father but I couldn't spot him. I was about to walk over to check on him again when my mother called out to me. And when I turned to see my family, father was with them, laughing with Imari and Karamu.

About two hours into the trek, a few of the youngsters complained their eyes were stinging. We'd all been struggling with the intense heat, but we're all pretty used to these conditions. However today, the dust was being kicked up far more than usual.

Father spotted a familiar outcrop of rock and was visibly agitated. He pushed his way through the crowd and headed towards it, charging his way past everyone without caring who he knocked into. As he reached the outcrop, he climbed to the highest point.

'Talib!' he called to one of his oldest friends, a Zebra from the north. 'Talib, try to slow everyone down, we are moving too quickly.' Talib was nearer the front of the group and heard my father's calls.

Father called to the entire herd, urging them to slow down and save their energy. But nobody reacted. He called again, much louder this time, and in his anger stamped his hoof on the rocky surface which echoed across the plain like thunder. But still the herd ignored his calls.

He looked to us as we were nearing and told us to keep going; he needed to speak to Talib urgently. As he jumped down from rock to rock, he lost his balance, falling from about half way down. Karamu screamed but mother quickly calmed her when father got back to his hoofs. Father was limping as he charged on toward the front of the sea of bodies and he soon disappeared through the dusty haze.

Gradually the pace of the herd slowed and the pain in my legs from trying to keep up was finally disappearing. When father returned, he told us Talib and the other leaders were going to spread out at the front to keep the herd moving at the slower pace. Mother asked if he was hurt, so he reassured her he was fine and that he would be able to just walk it off, but I could see blood on his back leg, from a small wound above his hock.

I went over to father to see if he was ok, 'I am fine son; it would take more than a small cut to slow me down,' he smiled.

'What was happening?'

'It is born into us to follow each other to safety. We have evolved to keep ourselves safe and we do this by maintaining this large group. When those at the front of the herd move faster, we instinctively follow to remain together, even if we don't realise we are doing it. Those at the front had been pushing on towards the west; they were excited because of the storms. I had to slow them down or they would have tired too quickly.'

'But isn't it better to get there sooner if the food will be more plentiful?'

'If it was guaranteed, yes, but if we use all of our energy now and find the storms have not been so fruitful? What then? We would be far worse off than we are now. We could be too weak to continue. One mistake could put the entire herd in danger.'

'This is why you're such a good leader father.'

'There are some among us that don't think so Berko. There are some that wish for change.'

Father has been revered for his strength and authority for years, and has always been trusted by the leaders of all the troops. Many of the elders even come to father for guidance, despite them being the true leaders of this entire herd. But father never rules them. He has always asked the other leaders for their guidance and he only makes decisions if it will benefit everyone.

Our herd is large, we wildebeest make up the majority with around one and a half million of us, and then there are all of our friends added to that. Because it would be too difficult to lead so many, the herd is divided into different groups that we call droves. They move along the same route, just a little behind so they can benefit from the stimulated growth of the grass we cause by treading and grazing it as we go. All of these droves have their own leaders and elders, and although they all come together quite often to talk and to share information, they normally stay to lead their own drove. It is only during our time within certain areas, like in the birthing grounds for example, that we all meet up and mingle throughout most of our stay. It gives us a chance to forge new friendships and to catch up with loved ones we don't see so much of on our journey.

Our drove has a number of leaders who all work with my father under the guidance of Idriis and Hekima, our elders. Like Talib; he is from a long, important line of zebra and is highly respected for his guidance and foresight. Father's always valued Talib's knowledge of the Serengeti, and they've worked well as a team for many years, as well as being very close friends. Then there's Afia, one of the fastest gazelle my father has ever known, she leads through her quick thinking and intelligence. She's a close friend of my mother and Mbali, and her husband Hasan and their daughter Khola often spend time with our family when she is carrying out her duties as a leader. Jelani and father have grown up together, and they are more like brothers than friends. They were inseparable as children, much like Ayana and me, and now they love working together for the herd too. And then finally there's Kwame, a giant eland, and he really lives up to this, making everyone else seem tiny in comparison. He and father became friends when they were adolescents, and have always been especially close since Kwame saved father from one of our enemies. Mother told me that when Father was younger, he was ambushed by a leopard while taking a drink from a stream. Kwame spotted the leopard in the grasses just in time, and as she jumped up at father and grabbed him around the neck, Kwame leapt in, catching both the leopard and my father with his antlers. Kwame's right antler punctured the leopard's chest causing her to release father immediately and run into the long grass screaming in agony. But his left antler punctured the flesh of father's shoulder, leaving a large cut and now a prominent scar. Kwame felt awful for injuring his good friend, but father cherishes that scar. To him it is a mark of true friendship, and a constant reminder that you should never become complaisant on the Savannah. Despite being leaders and having the most important roles within our drove, the bond my father shares with all of them and the closeness of their friendships is what makes them work so well together.

At a slow canter the herd was far more comfortable. And there was less dust in the air, so visibility was much better, and it was much easier to breathe in the intense heat too. It also seemed like we'd get further than anticipated despite slowing the pace, because we were able to maintain that speed for much longer. And with the sun setting ahead of us, we'd be able to travel until later in the day, meaning we'd arrive at the river by dusk. This would still give us plenty of time to drink and rest, and hopefully feed too. And if the storms had been as rewarding as they appeared, then the small rivers and streams feeding the lakes would be flowing. These would come into view as we near the rift valley to the west, before the lake even brimmed the horizon. We've always used this as a resting place before heading on to the lake in the morning to set up camp. These have always been welcome signs for the herd, because we know the rivers and the lake will hold such promise.

The sun was lowering straight ahead of the herd and the detail of those up front dissolved as they became pure silhouettes against the beautiful ochre skyline. A ripple of sound flowed across the group and as it got louder it was a message from the front being passed down through. We were told the rivers were coming into view and flowing fresh and cold. The storms were as strong as predicted and our stay would be heavily rewarded. We quickly relayed the message to those behind, and the sound of voices passed back like a gust of wind through the grass.

The last time we travelled this way, we weren't lucky enough to see the rivers flowing. We had to continue to the lake, and it was the smallest it had been for many years. The edges of the lake were deep with sticky mud; the last of the water being sucked up by the heat of the sun. Some of the smaller animals among us were able to reach the edges of the lake without becoming stuck, but the majority had to go without. The leaders had a difficult choice; carry on in the hope the storms had provided for us further on, or turn back and head for the last full watering hole. But this would have been another day's trek and then we'd still have to turn again when this had dried up too. The elders and all the leaders made the decision to continue because we wildebeest can survive longer without water than any of the others, and with our vast numbers we could help our friends along if needed. The herd followed the decision and we all continued to the north. But the lack of water was soon apparent among some of the older members of the herd and their weakness was soon noticed by our enemies. There were many killings, which scarred the herd even to this day. My grandfather was among the casualties, taken by a pack of hyenas while trying to protect some of the youngsters. He tried his hardest to fight them off, but he was far too weak. Hekima and Idriis rushed the pack to disperse them all and they were able to get the youngsters to safety. But my grandfather couldn't get away. By the time my father and the other leaders arrived, it was too late. It's the reason father is so focused on the rains, and why he feels it's important to plan the herds' migration so meticulously this season.

After passing the message back, I craned my neck to look over the undulating mass of animals. Ahead of the furthest silhouettes, the rivers appeared like small cracks in the earth. Flashes of orange and bright yellow light danced and skated on the surface, and the reflections of the sky disappeared briefly as the breeze broke up the image and moved it around playfully. The sun danced on the water and as we neared, it moved along, guiding us towards our final reward. The river curved around and the sun disappeared beneath the bank, only to reappear mischievously on the other side of the bend. I was mesmerised by the light, and couldn't stop following the bright orange disc with my eyes. And as the small rivers converged and the banks began to widen, the horizon presented the most beautiful gift of all. The lake bubbled over the earth like a giant droplet from the edge of a leaf and the sun sat proudly above it, shimmering in on its ripples to show us what the morning had to offer. Flocks of tall pink birds were wading through the shallows darting left and right in synchronised patterns, and lining the banks were our good friends the buffalo, already there enjoying the riches that vast oasis had to offer.

The sun sank slowly beneath the lakes surface emitting a glow of pink light from below the horizon. It is only a few miles away, but our hike for the day was finally over. Thirsty and exhausted we could rest until morning, and know that our wishes had truly been granted.

We all had a chance to drink and the water tasted sweeter than ever. It was hard to stop drinking, even when the cold hurt my head. It was at the water's edge I finally saw Ayana again; I hadn't had a chance to speak to her since I was so rude to her. The dusk light was highlighting her face and as she drank, the pink light danced on the ripples formed by her lips. 'Sorry about this morning Ayana,' I said before she even noticed me.

'Oh hey Berko,' she looked up and gently shook the droplets from her chin. 'What are you sorry for?'

'I shouldn't have been so rude to you earlier. When you were playing with Imari and Karamu.'

'Rude? To be honest I didn't really notice,' she bent down to have another drink of the cold, sweet water. I felt thirsty too, but instead just stood watching her drink in the twilight.

'I was worried about my father. Like I said before he's been stressed about the journey and I was distracted by something he'd said.'

'Its fine, honestly, you don't have to explain yourself. It's natural to be tetchy when we start this journey. Most of the herd are snappier than usual. And I know it's been harder for you this season with your brother and sisters' arrival. Your parents have been a bit distracted looking after them. But it isn't down to you to worry about everything. Let your parents do the worrying. You're allowed to relax,' she gave me a gentle nudge. 'And act your age.'

'I know you're right of course... as always,' I nudged her back and she giggled. 'I guess I just feel I should help my mother out when my father is busy with his meetings.'

'Well, now the herd are finally together, the adults are far less anxious. And my mother said she is going to help with Imari and Karamu tomorrow. So you can walk with me if you like?'

'I would like that Ayana.'

We both had a drink together, and every now and then she looked up and smiled at me. And my own anxiety started to dissolve with the last of the evening light.

The following morning was like a miracle. We'd all gone to sleep feeling content having just drunk our weight in fresh water. We had all been talking among ourselves about the prospect of food to the north following these storms, which gave the group a further burst of energy and excitement. But when we awoke, we found we were sleeping by vast luscious grasslands, unlike any we had seen for months. The rains must have fallen early in the area this year and nourished the earth, but in the low light at our arrival and our pure excitement of the river, we didn't spot these grasslands. The new shoots were succulent and full of sweetness, and as we all ate our share, you could feel the energy flow over the herd.

The leaders decided it would be good for the herd to remain there for a while and set up camp, instead of moving on to the lake. The water was in good supply and there would be enough food for us all as long as we weren't greedy. Everyone agreed with this decision; we were all happy there and extremely comfortable. Although it was open and exposed, there were fewer places for our enemies to hide. The grasses were a little too short for them to ambush us and the land was flat, allowing us to see anyone coming for miles. It felt good there. And the herd felt safe.

We stayed in the area for several days before the leaders even started to discuss the prospect of moving on. It was the first time in years our herd had called the place home, and it was nice to hear the elders' stories about their last memories of it. During our stay, there were a number of rainstorms which just added to our comfort. The rivers were being filled up and in turn so were our bellies. The ground was soft and far more comfortable than what we'd been used to in the east, but above all, everyone was completely relaxed. And happy. I just wish we could have stayed forever, but I knew in my heart we would have to succumb to our instincts and move on again.

I was much happier, not just because of the constant supply of water and lush grass, or the great night's sleep I'd had on the soft ground. But I had actually been able to spend time with Ayana again. And after what she said the other day, I'd spent less time worrying about my father and more time "acting my age", as she says. I'll admit I do worry when I see my father looking troubled, because usually he's so strong. But in my heart I know he's able to cope with any situation he faces.

In truth I've been thinking more about myself recently than about anyone else. *And* the upcoming journey we are taking. When my siblings arrived I was really happy, excited even, because I was finally a big brother. And although my parents ask me to look after them quite often, I actually don't mind. In fact I really enjoy spending time with them both. But the more time I spent with them in the sacred lands, the more I thought about my own journey. I have tried my best to prepare them for what to expect, without scaring them too much, or putting them off. But while I was telling them about the fresh pastures and the many different animals we'll meet along the way, I was reminded that this was going to be my third journey. And that's why I have been a bit preoccupied.

Everyone else my age, including Ayana, has been really excited about this journey. It marks a huge turning point for us. This year we start our lessons with our parents and we learn all about the savannah. When we go through some physical changes over the course of this season, we will be given more independence and will finally be allowed to venture away from the herd because we will be perceived as mature and therefore viewed as adults. So everyone else my age is excited and enjoying their last few months of immaturity.

But I can't relax. Because when we are finally seen as adults, we are expected to forge our own path. And I will need to choose a lifestyle. We males can choose whether we want to build a harem with multiple females, join in a strong partnership with a single female, or a male if we are not interested in breeding, or to be a loner.

I will also need to decide if I want to stand out and prove my dominance, or just fade into the herd to travel with the others and follow the leaders every word. This isn't a bad existence by any stretch and it is the lifestyle chosen by the vast majority of the animals. It's actually quite satisfying to have your life lead from the front by somebody stronger, braver and more assertive than yourself. And it can be an extremely relaxing way of life, to just float along in the caravan across this vast expanse, and know that the decisions that help you survive are all being made for you. But of course, for many of the animals here it is easy to choose that life for themselves, because their parents did it, and their grandparents before them. But I am the son of Imamu. And despite all the woodlands and the deep valleys on this savannah, I have nowhere I can hide from my own fate.

My closest friends Akili and Suhuba stopped talking to me when our siblings were born because they too were aware of how important this season is for us all. I had an amazing bond with them both, but as soon as the adults started talking about us growing up, and choosing the paths we want to follow, they all just stopped hanging out with me. They even bullied me just to prove they're stronger than I am, or to show they also have what it takes to be a leader. They think I have an easy life because of who my father is. But it's not who *I* am. I've always found it difficult to speak up around anyone else, including my friends, because I'm not like my father. Or my grandfather either. I'm not brave, or wise. I can't give others support like my father can, or give advice on anything important. And I definitely don't have any authority; even my own siblings can run circles around me. But all this didn't matter. However much I told them all this, I still lost their friendship.

As the parents felt safe in the area the leaders had chosen, my siblings were able to go and play in the nursery group. So Ayana and I were able to have some time away from babysitting. It was good to get back to our old ways again. It was actually Ayana who taught me that true friendship means standing by someone through any situation. I have known her for as long as I can remember. She has always been there for me. And I have always been there for her too. Even when my other friends deserted me, she never did. She stood by me. Her friendship is something I cherish, and I know I always will. But recently it's started to feel different.

We've been talking far more about grown up things, like the hike and how fruitful the storms will be. And I don't know why, but I thought adults only talked like this because they had to, and I thought it would be boring when I finally had to be more serious. But with Ayana it's strange; I don't get bored of the conversations. In fact I've been trying to find more things to talk about so I have an excuse to hang out with her for longer. And the last couple of days, whenever it's time for her to go back with her parents, I've felt a bit lost. When we were young, I always wanted to stay out later if we hadn't finished a game or she had beaten me at Ampe. I don't know if it's because this area has given us more freedom than usual to spend far more time together, but now I don't want to be away from her at all.

Ayana and I were walking down by the river again today; we were talking about the next destination to the north-west. 'Do you think the woodlands will be better than here?' she said.

'I don't know. This place has been amazing, and it's been a long time since I've seen the herd this relaxed. It's hard to imagine anywhere being better than this.'

'I know. I feel at ease here too. I know we have to move on sooner or later, but I've enjoyed the time we've had here. And I've liked seeing the old Berko again. You've been a lot happier lately, you haven't been so distant. Or so boring,' she smiled wryly. 'I like this Berko.'

'I'm sorry again Ayana, I was so worried about my father that I kind of lost sight of my own life,' I lied. 'But after this week, I know the herd will have trust in him again.'

'You know, your father can handle this right? You don't need to carry his burdens. After all, he did lead us to this water,' she said, swirling her hoof on the surface, 'and it's the *coldest* water I've ever had,' she flicked the water into my face and laughed. I tried to splash her back, but she ran off too quickly. 'Too slow,' she called before looking back at me and giggling.

I chased after her, watching as she darted through the herd. I caught up as she came back out further down. As she turned, I accidently caught her back hoof and she tripped, falling softly on the ground. I stumbled and fell right on top of her and we both laughed. She looked right into my eyes and I found myself staring at her. She laughed again and then she kissed me on the cheek and said 'I like it when you're more relaxed Berko. You are much more fun.' She nudged me in the ribs playfully to get me off her, 'Berko?'

'Yes... sorry Ayana,' I smiled at her and quickly got up, helping her to her hoofs before we both shook the dust from our coats and laughed again about the whole thing.

We walked along the edge of the river to sit in the grass and we talked until the sun disappeared below the horizon. And we even found more things to talk about while we walked all the way back to the herd.

I couldn't sleep. I couldn't get that moment with Ayana out of my mind. I led there staring at the stars and focusing on every little noise around me. The older animals snoring in rhythmic melody. The young ones tossing and turning to get comfortable in their mothers embrace. Crickets chirping on the tips of tall grasses, and bats swooping and clicking as they hunted moths on the breeze. Every now and then a low rumble echoed through the herd and my stomach grumbled as if to reply. The grass had now become sparse and our occasional meals had been getting further apart every day, but with the peace and tranquillity there, and our ability to relax without fear, it was making it easy to overlook our hunger.

I heard the rumble again, but it was deep, and much louder than before. It resonated right through my chest. Looking across the herd, everyone was asleep, so I watched to make sure there was nothing unusual among them. The full moon lit the night sky with a pale blue glow that highlighted the herd with bright outlines. The entire herd was perfectly still and the savannah was serene in the early hours. Above the herd, just over the horizon, a flash of purple light created silhouettes of the distant trees. Relieved, I led back down and smiled as I pictured how lush the grasses will be when we reach those storms in a few weeks. Sometime after the flash I heard the low rumble again, and I could even hear a gentle splashing of water.

I must have drifted off at some point during the early hours because I was woken by my brother Imari at first light who was upset and scared. 'I had a scary dream Berko. Just after I went to sleep I dreamed there was a monster in the river, and when I woke up I heard a scary noise coming to get me.'

'It's ok, I heard it too,' I squinted at him and as my eyes focused I could see he was getting even more scared by my response. 'But you don't have to be scared Imari, it wasn't a monster. There were storms last night. The sounds of thunder must have got into your dreams.'

'Are you sure Berko?'

'I am certain. Honestly, you don't need to worry,' I touched my cheek to his and then I looked right at him. 'They were large storms, with lots of lightning, and it sounded like there was lots of rain too. So you know what that means?'

His eyes widened at the idea of fresh grass again, 'I'm going to go and wake up Karamu and tell her all about the storms,' he said excitedly and ran off shouting her name.

I sat up, the sun was hurting my eyes and I knew I wouldn't get back to sleep with all the noise the young ones were making, so I went to see my father who was looking over the herd checking numbers.

'Morning father' I said, making him jump. 'Sorry,' I whispered.

'Morning Ber... Are you ok my son? You don't look well,' he said looking at my half lidded eyes.

'I didn't get much sleep. I was focusing on the storm in the distance; it sounded like heavy rain too.'

'There is no sign of rain this morning I'm afraid.'

'No I mean in the distance. Over the horizon.'

'Really?' he said before smelling the breeze frantically. 'I better send Macaria to check it out.' He looked worried, but then he looked back at me and smiled. 'I feel like I have not seen much of you lately Berko, you look like you are growing taller. It is nice to see you spending more time with Ayana again; I know your siblings can be demanding, but your mother and I don't want you to neglect your friendship with her.'

'She's my best friend father; she stood by me when my friendship with Akili and Suhuba broke down.'

'I know,' he smiled at me. 'Well, true friendship means standing by each other through any situation that you face Berko. Your friendship with Ayana is very strong.'

I smiled to myself as he said this, remembering Ayana had only said this to me recently. I was about to leave when father stopped me again. 'You said you could hear rain last night, where was the noise coming from? I am struggling to sense any signs of it this morning Berko.'

'It sounded like it was coming from beyond the river, just behind the herd. I assumed it was echoing from the storms.'

He sniffed the breeze again. 'Be careful today Berko, ok?'

'OK.'

He went back to checking on the herd, but he had that same glazed look in his eye again.

I saw Ayana heading towards the riverbank. When I caught up I asked her how she'd slept and if she heard the thunder in the night, but she said she hadn't. I went with her down to the water's edge to have a drink. Some of the older animals had started to stir by now, some woken by the sunlight shining across the plain and others being woken by their children. But overall many of the herd were still sleeping, making the most of the relaxed atmosphere.

As Ayana and I reached the water, there were others from the herd lining the bank to drink. As I looked along the river, watching those taking a drink in the morning sunlight, I too felt relaxed, it was peaceful. I looked at Ayana and remarked on the serenity of the area and she looked around to take it all in.

As we were looking up stream I heard the rumble again. 'Did you hear that Ayana?'

She looked up, pricking her ears, trying to pinpoint where it was coming from. 'Yes I heard it that time,' she turned to me. 'Why do you look so worried?'

'I don't know. I think it's because it means we'll have to move on soon. Those storms have been rumbling for some time now, so the grasslands to the west could be far better than here. I guess I'm just sad to leave this place.'

'There hasn't been talk of moving yet.'

'No, but father was distracted again this morning. He must be making plans.'

I leant down to drink, and as I did I heard the rumble again. All of the others lining the bank stood up quickly, all hearing what I heard. I looked towards the horizon to see if the storm was heading towards us, but I couldn't see any rain. There wasn't a single cloud in the sky. Everyone looked as confused as I did, but then one of the elders along the bank said 'earth tremors are very common in this area, they can sometimes vibrate all the way from the rift valley,' so we all went back to having a drink and enjoying the peaceful morning.

As I lifted my head again and licked the droplets from my lips, I heard the rumble again, and this time the water was gently rippling and splashing ahead of us. I nudged Ayana and she stood up and watched it too.

The ripple appeared to move downstream as if caught in the current and then slowly dissolved into the water.

A young female gazelle came down to the water's edge a few meters along from where we were standing and raised her head to greet us both. As she leant down to take a drink of fresh cold water, the rumble returned, only much louder this time. She stood up and raised her head as we all did earlier, but when the noise subsided she returned to drink. As her lips got closer to the water, the surface danced and bubbled ahead of her. As she went to take another sip there was a huge splash, and that familiar rumble became almost deafening. The waters' surface exploded in front of the gazelle and a dark shape came bursting through the spray, like a lightning bolt tearing through the clouds. There was a loud screech from the poor gazelle as she was snatched from where she stood and disappeared beneath the surface in a blink.

There was a furore all around us of those who'd all seen what just happened; everyone was trying desperately to get up the bank, pushing each other aside to get a better grip in the dirt.

Ayana was frozen to the spot, staring straight into the water, her legs trembling with fear. Ahead of her, the surface started to ripple and a wake of water was heading straight for her. Just as I got to the water's edge, the surface erupted loudly, and I barged Ayana away from the danger. Something brushed my back leg as I ushered Ayana up the bank, but when I looked back it had already disappeared beneath the surface again.

Along the bank, the gazelle had resurfaced and was splashing around in the shallows, trying desperately to get to the edge, 'I need to help her,' I shouted, but

Ayana grabbed my tail in her teeth and stopped me from going back.

Another loud splash erupted from the water, spraying us both and the gazelle was dragged back in by a dark, scaly shape. The creature spun with the gazelle in its jaws and then as I saw it's pale, ridged belly, I shielded Ayana's gaze. The gazelle was pulled beneath the surface as two more creatures came over to wrestle for their share. By the time Ayana and I got up the bank, there was no sign of the gazelle, just red, brown foam swirling on the water's surface and the nauseating rumble from deep beneath the current.

The news had already made it to the rest of the herd and there was panic all around us as father and the other leaders were trying desperately to calm everyone down.

Ayana was now shaking all over with fear of what we'd just witnessed. 'What... what was that Berko?' She said with a tremble in her voice.

'I don't know Ayana. I don't know.'

'You... you were going to... to go back. You... you could have been killed.'

'I know. I just wanted to help her...' I paused to hold back a tremble in my own voice. 'Come on, we need to find our families and let them know we're safe.'

There was so much confusion among the group; they were running around, trying desperately to find their loved ones. Although only a few of us saw what happened, it was as if the entire herd already knew about it. I told Ayana to stay close while we fought through the crowds, I didn't want to lose her too. I was shouting for animals to move and had to shove some of them aside as we went. A female gazelle stopped us and asked if I'd seen her daughter in the crowds, I shook my head but couldn't look at her, 'I'm so sorry...' I said, 'I have to find my family.' Ayana took hold of my tail in her teeth so she didn't lose me and I guided her along. I spotted Mbali and then noticed my family with her. We got through to them and when Mbali saw us she and my mother ran over to us. 'Oh thank the Stars you are OK.' Mbali cried, looking upwards to the skies. 'When I heard what happened, I was terrified. I knew you were going to get a drink and then I saw the panic over by the river. They were saying one of the children was caught by a crocodile,' she said.

'It... it was one of the gaz... gazelles,' Ayana said and she broke down as Mbali tried to comfort her.

'Was she?' mother whispered to me, knowing I would understand her question. I just nodded slowly to confirm the news and mother dropped her head in empathy. 'Poor child.'

Imari asked what was happening so I said I'd tell him later. I knew once the commotion had died down, he would have forgotten all about it. I don't think his young fragile mind could accept what I saw. I'm not even sure I can.

A little later that morning when calmness had returned to the herd, the leaders called a meeting. Father and the others stood on a large flat rock in the middle of the grassland and the herd swarmed around them like flies. Father made an announcement.

'The leaders have been discussing the storms to the north-west and we have decided the herd should start heading north in the morning. We have stayed here longer than originally scheduled and we need to move on if we are to make it to our next stop within the month.'

There was a wave of voices flowing around the herd and then one voice shouted with real ferocity.

'So all of a sudden you've decided we should move on? I wonder what caused that decision!' The chatter within the herd then got louder and Idriis shouted for silence.

'We always had this plan in place,' said father. 'We just took the opportunity given to us by the stars to stay at the rivers instead of moving on to the lake. We have followed this route and this schedule for millennia and it is not for us to change it. The leaders have collectively decided we should head forth and aim for the grasslands to the north. It is nearing the time of Masika, when the long rains will start. We should arrive in time for the fresh crop of grasses and flowers, and these will help us to build our strength for the Rut.'

'Imamu is right,' said Talib. 'We have had enough time to rest, but we haven't had the nutritious meals we require. The lush grass to the north will give us all the strength we need and it will ensure our offspring benefit too. They need the energy for the harsh winter months, but they cannot get that here.'

'So this has nothing to do with the attack this morning!' shouted the same voice as before; it was Hatari, an adult wildebeest who had been exiled from the herd years ago. He was barging his way to the front.

Father stepped forward and spoke quietly towards Hatari, 'you have no right to be here Hatari, and you have no right to try and spread fear among the youngsters. What happened was a tragedy and it was not foreseen by any of us. And why is moving on such a bad thing when it is for the safety of the herd?' He looked back up to address the crowd. 'As Talib said, we need to prepare for the harsh months ahead. But we can only do that if we move on. What happened today was awful and it has shaken the entire herd, but we will not let it decide our fate for us. That is why we are not leaving until the morning as scheduled.'

There was a cheer from the crowd in support of my father and then they all bowed their heads in respect for Duni, the young gazelle.

Hatari turned back to face the crowd and called out again with rage in his voice. 'You are all pathetic! You all love "The Great Imamu" but can't you see he is steering you wrong? He is leading us all to slaughter. That young gazelle won't be the first, you mark my words. She was just the start!' He spat on the ground and turned to face the leaders, bowing sarcastically towards my father.

'Get back to the edges of the herd Hatari; you were exiled for a reason. You are disrespectful,' shouted Jelani. Hatari turned and smirked before walking away. In his anger, Jelani tried to confront Hatari but my father stopped him.

'Let him go Jelani,' said father, 'his opinions are his own. And this breach of his sentence will not help his case.'

Idriis stepped forward and addressed the herd once again. 'Please do not listen to Hatari; his words have no validity here. Many of you know of his past. And his attitude towards us all. Please, go back to the grasslands and feed as much as you can in preparation for the morning. But take great care going down to the river to drink.'

The leaders all bowed their heads to indicate the meeting was over and everyone started to walk away. I could hear the chatter through the group, mostly in support of the leaders, but every now and then I could hear father's name and when I was recognised they would stop talking. I wanted to speak with father, but I knew he would be too busy talking with other herd members, so I went back to find my family.

Mother was telling my siblings to only go for water with her. I just sat down in the short grass and closed my eyes, but as hard as I tried, I couldn't get the images of this morning out of my mind.

At dawn the herd started for the north at a muted pace. There was an air of sadness over the entire group for the family of the gazelle; she was only having a drink in the early light. Her mother would have thought nothing of it; she would have been as relaxed as the rest of us.

I was sad to be leaving this area, until yesterday it had been a happy and relaxed place, so to leave it after all this time was upsetting. But above all I felt guilty. I was there. I could have helped her get back out of the river. But I stood there and watched as she tried desperately to clamber out, only to be dragged back in. I couldn't sleep last night with the images going through my head. And all I could hear was that awful rumbling sound.

Further along the journey, the feeling of guilt got even stronger when I kept going over everything in my mind. I'd heard the rumbling all that time; it kept me awake the night before. I even mentioned it to father but I'd been so preoccupied with my thoughts of Ayana that I didn't do anything about it. I could have prevented this from even happening if I'd just told father what I'd

CHASING THE RAIN

really heard. I needed to talk to him. He always knows what to say.

When I caught up to father, he had that glazed look again and I didn't know if I should burden him with my own worries. But then he caught sight of me and he smiled. 'Berko, I am so happy to see you my son. I am sorry I haven't spoken to you much. Mother told me about the river yesterday. Are you ok?'

'I can't stop seeing it father. I wanted to help her. I should have helped her. I was right there and I did nothing. I feel awful.'

'What would you have done Berko? Other than risk being dragged in yourself?' he looked right at me. 'You did what you should have done, you got yourself to safety. And I hear from Jelani that you even got Ayana to safety too. He was very proud of you when she told him that.'

'But the gazelle father, I didn't get her to safety.'

'That is not your fault son; you must never think it was. There are times to be brave and you were brave for Ayana. Guiding her to safety took a lot of courage,' he touched his cheek to mine. 'Risking your own life to save that gazelle would have been foolish. The crocodile that took her wouldn't have been alone Berko, there would have been others.'

'I saw another two fighting to drag her under as I walked away.'

'Then you were sensible to leave. I couldn't face losing you Berko. Don't ever think you have to be a hero, do you hear me?'

'Yes father. I still feel guilty though. I should have told you about the noise I'd heard. When you asked, I told you it was the storm.'

41

Father looked down solemnly. 'It is I who should feel guilty Berko. When you told me about the sound, I had a bad feeling. It's why I told you to be careful. I know our enemies often stay within the Lake of Masek, to the west, I have seen them for myself in the past and my father always told me to be careful when we stayed there. But they must have swum up the river when we outstayed our welcome this season. I should have moved the herd on sooner, this could have all been avoided. So maybe Hatari was right, maybe it was my fault.'

'Hatari is a bully Father! He's been jealous of you since you were young, mother told me. You can't let someone like Hatari cloud your judgement; you've never made a mistake for this herd. And you never will.'

Father touched his cheek to mine. 'Thank you Berko, you always know the right things to say. You are going to make a fine leader my son.' I stopped dead in my tracks. 'Are you ok Berko?' Father asked as he stopped to look back at me.

'Um, yes,' I said hesitantly. 'I... I just remembered I told Ayana I'd meet with her. I have to go. I'll catch up with you later father.'

'Ok, see you later Berko.'

I lost sight of father as I headed back in the opposite direction, ducking and swerving though the herd. I was exhausted so I had to stop and rest. I knew I'd be able to catch up to my family at the slow pace the herd was moving. I was being shoved and knocked as everyone walked by, so I pushed my way out through the group and headed to the open plain.

I was feeling dizzy and had to sit for a minute, I walked to the shade of a rocky outcrop overlooking the river; I was tired but I also had thoughts whizzing around my brain. What did father mean? Could he really see me as a leader? I couldn't make decisions for a herd of this size. I can't even make the right decision for myself. I'm immature, I'm selfish. I might disagree about this when I argue with mother, but she is basically right. I'm not ready to lead. I'm barely ready to grow up.

I'd been sat in the shade for a while and when I finally looked up I'd lost sight of the herd. Panic started to set in. Worried I could end up lost out here, and it is never a good idea to be alone on the savannah, I tried to work out the direction the herd was heading. The top of the outcrop I was sat beside would give me a better vantage point, so I headed round the rocks to look for a way to climb up. As I came out from the shade, I heard hoof steps and voices. I recognised one of the voices and as they got closer I could make out what they were saying.

It was Hatari and a group of adolescent males from our troop. He was walking in front of them and kept turning back to talk to them all, telling them how funny it was to rile the leaders up. Then he was talking about getting rid of all of them. 'Imagine, we could have longer rests, more water and the best grazing patches on the grasslands. We would have all of the power and our choice of females. The herd would bow to us, not Imamu or that retched Talib. Who does he think he is telling us how we should live? We are wildebeest; we should travel with wildebeest, not Zebra. And definitely not a Nyumbu like him.' The younger males were hanging on every word, laughing as he mocked Talib and all the other troops.

Father and Talib have been friends for years and all our troops have been friends for centuries. We don't see the other animals as any different to us; we only see each other as a herd. So to hear talk like this made me feel sick all over again. I knew I had to tell my father what I'd heard, but I needed to get to them without being seen by Hatari or his followers. Our next rest stop was at Lake Masek and I remembered what father had said; that the crocodiles must have swum up this river from the lake. So I slowly and quietly walked down to the riverbank to follow it towards the lake. That way I'd be able to sneak past Hatari unseen and catch up to the herd further downstream. But I knew there were dangers lying in these waters. So I had to be fast, but above all, I had to stay safe.

I slid down the dry, crumbling bank on a wave of dust and gravel. I followed the river, slowly at first; I didn't want Hatari or the others to hear me below them. When I was far enough ahead, I picked up the pace.

I cantered along the riverbank, dodging large clumps of dried mud and jumping over rocks and dead branches jutting out of the dirt. As my hoofs hit the ground, the sundried crust cracked and I sank slightly into the softer mud beneath, my hoofs squelching as they sucked back out. My rhythmic stride reverberated down to the water, and as I ran that unmistakable rumble started to follow me.

Further ahead the river turned sharply to the right and as I got closer, I could hear that terrifying sound getting louder and louder; it was racing me down the river to cut me off at the bend. My heart was pounding with fear and exhaustion, but I had to keep going. I glanced to my left and the water rippled and undulated like a huge serpent.

Fatigued but pumped full of adrenaline, I pushed my legs to move faster than they ever have before. I galloped along the bank, leaping over a large root sticking out of the soil, and the shallow water beside me came to life. There were crocodiles everywhere, with a throng of teeth and bodies thrashing and sloshing in the water and silt. I turned quickly to my right, digging my hoofs in to make the tight turn, and then I tore up the bank, to get to safer ground. The bodies were scrambling one over the other to catch me, but they got caught up on each other which slowed them down.

I lost my hoofing at the top of the bank and a large clump of dirt broke free and tumbled down to the water's edge. As it hit the surface, the river bubbled and splashed and the tangle of bodies churned angrily once again. I spotted the mass of the herd in the distance and took a deep breath as I dug my hoofs in to pull myself up onto solid ground.

My heart was trying to tear though my chest, but I couldn't stop now. The river was dangerous enough, but to be out here alone is much, much worse.

'Ayana!' I called, weaving through the dense crowd of animals. 'Ayana, can I speak to you?'

'Berko, what's wrong?'

'I need to talk to you,' I said through heavy breaths and led her away from her family as quickly as I could.

'What is it?'

'I've just seen Hatari, with Thairu and his friends. I had to run along the riverbank so they wouldn't see me.'

'Berko, you could have been killed.'

'He was mocking Talib, and his little followers were making disgusting comments about all our friends.' She was more shocked when I said this than of anything else, even my near death experience.

'You need to tell your father. The leaders need to know.'

We walked for a while in complete silence. I wanted to tell her about the comment my father had made earlier, of me making a great leader, but I didn't want her to think I was being arrogant. A couple of times I went to speak. About normal things, like I usually do. But every time I opened my mouth I just froze. After what felt like ages Ayana finally broke the silence. She put her cheek to mine and whispered 'thank you,' in my ear.

'What for?' I said confused, and partly worried I'd said something out loud without knowing it.

'What do you think? For saving my life Berko.'

'Oh... Well I didn't exactly save your life Ayana. I just helped you up the bank.'

'I would have been killed if you didn't act the way you did. I couldn't move when I saw that poor young gaz...' she paused for a while, and then took a deep breath. 'I was terrified. I just froze when that other crocodile was coming straight towards me. But you didn't even stop to think. You got me away from there. You didn't even think of your own safety.'

'I didn't really do anything Ayana. Anyone would have done the same thing.'

'Berko, there were about fifteen others along that bank. They all just ran to safety. Even that older wildebeest who was right next to Duni got away as quickly as he could. You were brave Berko.'

'I was scared too, even if I didn't show it. I was scared you would get hurt. I don't know what I would've done if that was you.' She pressed her cheek to mine again.
'I... I better find my father and tell him about Hatari,' I said hastily, feeling my face warming up with embarrassment. 'I'll catch up soon Ayana, OK?'

'OK Berko. Let me know what happens.'

'I will.'

When I caught up to my father, he was talking with Kwame, Talib and Jelani. 'But it's coming up to five years Imamu. His sentence is almost up,' pleaded Kwame passionately.

'Well he isn't showing any signs he has changed. I've had three members of the herd tell me they've seen him walking through the group, and two others have told me he's been spreading rumours about the leaders. Come on Imamu, you have to convince Idriis. He can't let him rejoin the herd, not after breaking the rules of his sentence. And especially after his display at the meeting this morning,' added Jelani.

'I have heard rumours too,' said father. 'And I have even been questioning my own leadership after hearing some of the whispers around the herd recently.'

'What? You know the herd have complete trust in you Imamu. You cannot let Hatari get under your skin,' said Kwame. 'His rumours will soon diminish, and the herd will see right through him.'

'But there is no evidence these untruths have come from Hatari.'

'There is nobody else that underhoofed in this herd Imamu,' said Kwame.

'Many of the herd were hurt by his actions, and they all know his sentence is coming to an end so they would say anything to try and keep him on the outskirts.'

'Even so Imamu, Kwame is right. This does seem like the behaviour of Hatari,' said Jelani. 'And it is exactly the reason you need to ask Idriis to prevent him coming back.'

'You all know my thoughts on him, I would rather see him exiled from the savannah for what he did, but you know it is not down to me. Or any of us for that matter. It is the law of the herd, and Hatari has carried out his sentence.'

'Talib, he wronged you most of all,' said Jelani. 'Surely you don't want him back in this herd?'

'I made my mind up about Hatari long ago. Like Imamu, I would like to see him ejected from the savannah, and far from any of us. But it is the law of the herd. He has served his sentence. So if the elders decide he can return, then I will have to accept their decision.'

'I just don't trust him,' said Jelani. 'If he is spreading rumours just before his hearing, then he is being disrespectful of the herd's values. And as I said, he isn't showing that he has changed at all.'

'I will speak to the elders when we reach our next camp and tell them of our concerns,' said father. 'And I will remind them of his original crime. But all we can do is wait for their decision,' he said apologetically. But the other leaders didn't look happy.

I backed off and slipped out of sight behind a group of eland. If I told them what I'd heard, they'd never believe me. And to be honest I wouldn't want to repeat it, especially when Talib was with them.

We finally made it to the grasslands near the three lakes, just as the sun kissed the tops of the tallest mountains. This area has been a welcome stop for us all since the beginning of our species. It offers us another opportunity to rest for a couple of days and to refuel. The short grasses here are abundant and highly nutritious; they help us build our energy for the next stage of the journey. The herd often spread far and wide, covering as much area as we choose to make the most of the luscious pastures. The lakes provide ample water for all of us, and the chance to bathe, soothing the aches in our joints, cleaning our coats of dust and washing wounds and insect bites. But everyone seems much more hesitant than usual to enter the lake; the fright at the river is still haunting us all. We younger animals have learned a valuable lesson now to stay wary of the water. Not only to beware of drowning, but to watch for hidden dangers beneath its surface. We are taught of the dangers at the larger rivers to the north, and we are warned to be wary at the lakes too. Attacks happen often and we've learned to come up with strategies to avoid it, although our friends and family members do get taken. But what happened to Duni took us all by surprise. It hit the herd hard. I think it was the panic caused by those who ran that made things worse. It struck fear into the younger members of the herd and made it difficult for the leaders to regain calmness. Hopefully the few days we spend here will help the youngsters relax and start to have fun again. Although they've not been told any details of what happened, they need to learn that awareness of your surroundings doesn't mean living in constant fear.

I caught up with Ayana on the evening and we spoke more about Hatari. 'I couldn't tell him Ayana, the leaders were all talking about him. Apparently his sentence is up and he may be allowed back in. Father said he has to wait for the elders' decision, but after his recent behaviour, it seems unlikely he'll be let back in.'

'But if you'd told them, they might be able to stop him rejoining the herd.'

'They'd never believe me Ayana, they've had others tell them of the things he's done; my father is unsure who is telling the truth and who is lying as a way to persuade the council not to let him return. The leaders would just assume I'm making it up too, for Talib's sake. Besides, it could have been all talk by Hatari just to impress his young followers.'

'If they're impressed by that then they're far worse than I thought. And I don't trust Thairu, especially after the way he used to treat you.'

'I don't like Hatari, and I've never really liked Thairu either, he was a bully when we were younger and from what I heard earlier, he's still a bully now,' I could see Ayana was getting more uneasy at the thought of Hatari returning and influencing Thairu and his friends. What if we get up early tomorrow and spend the morning searching for Hatari. If we see him enter the herd, or hear him say anything that could prove he is breaking his sentence, then I'd be able to tell the leaders. They'd have to do something.'

She smiled widely and then touched her cheek to mine. 'Thank you Berko.'

When I used to see Hatari on the outskirts of the herd, I felt sorry for him. He'd always look sad when he was sat in the distance watching us all. When I grew a little older, mother told me all about him so I wouldn't hang around with the wrong kind of animals or make the same kind of choices he did.

Hatari was always badly behaved when he was young, and he seemed to take an instant dislike to Talib, trying to start fights with him all the time and even physically threatening him when they were my age. As he got older his attitude and behaviour got even worse. Mother says she was never comfortable to be around him because he'd often make disrespectful comments to her, Nakato and Mbali. He was always trying to impress them, but his comments did the complete opposite. My father and Jelani never really got along with him either. And the older they got, the more they tried to avoid him. He was always jealous that my mother was interested in my father and not him, and he would often make comments that she should be with a real wildebeest instead.

Hatari's parents weren't around; his father was killed shortly after his birth and his mother was sadly taken by a lioness during his second journey. When my parents began their lessons, he was due to start his with Idriis, who the other elders felt would be able to bring out his best side, but he soon started to bully the others in the group.

He was given a number of chances to change and to take part in the group lesson, but he always ruined it for himself by fighting with his classmates. Idriis was desperate to change him and he even promised to teach him away from the others. He spent a lot of time with Hatari, and treated him more like a son than a student. But even this wasn't enough to change his attitude. And when Idriis finally thought he'd made some progress, he caught him picking on a group of zebra who were much younger than him. Idriis called a meeting and it was publically announced that Hatari was not to be given any further lessons by anyone. And when he told the herd what Hatari had been calling them all, everyone was disgusted.

My grandfather and the other elders saw a lot of promise in father and Jelani, so they began to teach them the knowledge of the herd. They would take them out and teach them how to read the signs that tell us when to move on, how to smell the rain on the wind and how to spot signs of danger. Hatari soon got jealous of them, and he would often ask them what they'd been taught. When they didn't tell him he'd usually threaten them in his usual aggressive manner. They learnt to just ignore Hatari, and although this often made him angrier, it seemed to work and he'd soon walk away in a huff.

Later he started hanging around with two younger wildebeest, and because they looked up to him, he felt more powerful, so over time he stopped pestering my father and his friends and focused on bossing them around instead.

My father showed strength and wisdom and the herd just turned to him for anything, so naturally he was confirmed a leader. But after his ceremony Hatari got angry and tried to cause trouble. He started a fight, but focused his anger towards Talib, injuring him with his horns. The elders put him in his place and again, publicly announced what he'd done to show that he was deceitful. The majority of the herd gave up on him at this point, but his group of young followers were still as loyal as before.

My grandfather once said "individuals like Hatari don't possess the qualities needed to be a strong and trustworthy leader. You must be able to put others needs ahead of your own, not use the herd to make you look better." He didn't like Hatari, saying he had a dark spirit about him. That is something that follows us all; we have spirit guides that steer us in the direction written for us in our stars. Those with dark spirits will disobey their stars and try to rewrite their own destiny. There are members of the herd, some of the elders and even Talib, who read these spirits and let us know what our destiny foretells. The day my father was born, an elder told his parents they had just given birth to a very special son. They were told he would be strong and a highly revered leader. He was named Imamu to reflect his destiny. Some don't believe in the spirits, but my father is an example they must be true.

Ayana and I spent the rest of the evening talking. We were up until quite late and I finally told her what father had said to me. 'I feel he is just trying to make me feel better Ayana.'

'Your father wouldn't say it if he didn't mean it Berko. You are showing real maturity. My father was really impressed the other day too, saving me like that. And he said you remind him of your father. You need to believe in yourself Berko. I can see it, and so can others.' She moved closer to me.

'I don't know. I don't feel ready to be responsible for thousands of others. I don't feel I'm sensible enough to even look after my siblings.'

'Your father was just saying you show signs of a good leader. He isn't expecting you to do it tomorrow. You worry over the smallest things.'

'Exactly my point Ayana. I worry all the time, and I over think every little thing.'

'But that just shows you have the awareness of a great leader Berko. You won't be made leader over night,' she smiled and then yawned. 'You should be ready by the following day Berko,' she laughed. 'Try and get to sleep. We need wake up at first light if we are going to find Hatari.'

I thought about what she'd said and then about our task in the morning. 'Good night Ayana,' I said, but she had already drifted off. I stared up at the stars and tried to read what they were telling me, but they just looked like a bunch of little dots to me.

We set off quietly at dawn, trying not to disturb all those sleeping around us. We walked to the lake and Ayana drank while I kept watch for danger. She drank for ages without a break, and when she'd finished she said how she hadn't had a drop of water since that day because she was so scared. I touched my cheek to hers to comfort her before she kept watch while I had a drink.

We walked quietly around the herd and looked at everyone and within every group, in case Hatari was hiding among them. Most of the herd were starting to stir, so the two of us walking around didn't look so strange.

Hatari's sentence means he isn't actually allowed to enter the herd; he should remain on the outskirts for its entirety and can only set foot inside once the sentence has been lifted by the council of elders. Being exiled to the outskirts of the herd is a punishment that's only been used a couple of times throughout our history. Being very social, and always very wary of our enemies, we thrive within a herd, surrounded by our friends and loved ones. So being forced to follow as an outsider, with no interaction with anyone and being at constant risk of attack is the worst punishment any of us could imagine. This is why it is reserved only for members who have carried out the worst crimes towards another member of the herd. But Hatari has been flouting his sentence recently, by both attending the recent meeting, and mixing with Thairu and his friends. This should be enough to lengthen his sentence. But I need to be able to prove the latter to my father and the other leaders.

We spotted Hatari, sat in the open near the edge of the group and we stood among the adults to graze. As he stretched in the morning light, we watched to see if he spoke to anyone. He soon headed over to Thairu and the group of adolescents and gave them all a kick. 'Wake up you lazy oafs,' he shouted at them all.

Ayana turned to me and whispered 'they were all down by the river. The day the gazelle was taken.'

'Are you sure?'

'Definitely, I recognise the two on the left.'

I didn't want Hatari or Thairu to spot me so I turned my back to them all. I asked Ayana to relay what they were doing and listened out to hear what they were talking about. We stayed there for ages, just waiting for him to say anything we could tell the leaders, but we both knew it was a long shot. And when we tried to think about what his intentions might be, our imaginations got away from us.

Trying to look natural and eke out the grazing was difficult, so we were about to give up when another of the adolescents came charging through the herd towards Hatari. 'Sir, Imamu is going to be on watch today, when the sun is at its highest. He will be all by himself near the lake. That might be your best chance,' he said through heavy breaths.

'Good work. Now go and find me a good spot to graze.'

Ayana and I started to walk away slowly so we wouldn't draw attention to ourselves. But when we got behind a large group of zebra and out of sight, we ran as fast as we possibly could. When we got back to the herd, we couldn't find my father or any of the leaders anywhere.

Ayana and I spent the rest of the morning sitting in the sun waiting to catch sight of my father or Jelani. We'd both eaten too much fresh grass whilst watching Hatari to go on searching for them. While we waited, I told Ayana all the stories my mother had told me about Hatari.

'He used to be horrible to all of them when they were young, including the youngsters from the other troops, but my mother said he would aim most of his hatred towards Talib. He even tried to hurt him when they were Imari's age. They were all playing Mbube-Mbube. But when it was Hatari's turn to be the lion, he cheated. He pretended to keep his eyes closed. The others were calling Mbube as he got further away but instead of following their voices, Hatari kept heading straight towards Talib. He lunged out for him and caught Talib's front leg with his horns, tripping him over. The others shouted at him but he stood over Talib and threatened him. He put his hoof on Talib's throat. Everyone had to physically push Hatari off him, but he just said he was messing around and Talib shouldn't be such a cry baby. The older they got, the less they hung around with him and he made friends with two younger wildebeest. Mother said he used to boss them around and get them to save him the best grazing spots. He would always say things to them quietly whenever they walked past our fathers and their friends and would often mock Talib, calling him the little baby and laughing.'

'So he's always been nasty then!'

'Like they say Ayana, a leopard never changes its spots.'

'So when was he exiled to the outskirts?'

'It was shortly after Talib was made a leader. He'd always been jealous he wasn't chosen. On the evening of Talib's swearing in ceremony, Hatari came over to congratulate him. He was being strangely civil, but as he walked away he remarked that the herd should never have chosen a...' I paused.

'A what? Berko?'

I swallowed hard, 'a Nyumbu!' I said as quietly as I could.

'Oh my stars!'

I shook my head in both disgust and remorse for saying the word. 'Both our fathers and Kwame confronted him, but Talib told them to let it go. Then Hatari accused them of being Msaliti's for sticking up for a...' I refused to repeat that word again, 'so Talib stepped forward to confront him. To demand an apology. Hatari spat in Talib's face and said he would never apologise to a... you know... as long as he lived. Then he butted him and cut his face. That's how he got that scar. Father told me Talib was lucky not to lose his eye that day, and he almost had to forfeit his place with the leaders that year too. Idriis and Hekima were coming over to congratulate Talib and saw the whole thing. Hatari was ordered to attend a public meeting and after hearing all of the details, including all of his past behaviour, the herd voted for exile. He didn't really have any friends to back him up; the two wildebeest he used to hang around with fought him for dominance years ago, so he was always on his own after that. He had one son with a younger female who didn't know of his past, but she soon met a stronger, more dominant male and left Hatari so she could join that male's harem. His son doesn't even have much to do with him these days either, so I guess that's why he's trying to hang around with the young impressionable males. At least when his sentence is up he'll have someone on his side.'

'I have no sympathy for him at all.'

'I know, I kind of felt sorry for him when I used to see him following the herd alone, but when my mother told me those stories, that sympathy soon diminished.'

We went down to the lake to have a drink; the heat of the sun was becoming unbearable in the open. While Ayana was drinking I noticed her shadow was almost directly beneath her. 'Father will be on watch soon Ayana,' I said. She shook her head to flick the water from her chin and licked her lips and we headed over to where father would be.

Father was stood at the edge of the herd, near the large lake watching over the entire drove. He kept looking off to the horizon and smelling the breeze. Before I could call out to him, Hatari appeared from around the herd and was walking up to father. There was a group of older wildebeest napping in the sun so Ayana and I led between them so we could watch.

Hatari bowed his head to my father. 'Imamu, can I speak with you?' he said quietly.

'You are breaching your sentence yet again Hatari. Can you not see I am busy keeping watch over the herd? Can this not wait?' my father said without looking at him.

'I would like to speak now Imamu if I may? I won't keep you from your duties.' He spoke softly, almost submissively.

'Ok Hatari, but make this quick, I don't have time to argue.'

'That's what I want to speak to you about. I wanted to apologise for my outburst the other day at the meeting. It was wrong of me to do that.'

'It was disrespectful Hatari. We had just lost Duni, her mother Efia was distraught. The entire herd was grieving and you decided to challenge my leadership. Besides, your apologies are empty. You are merely trying to lift the burden of guilt from your own shoulders.'

'I mean it Imamu. I promise.'

'As I said Hatari, I don't wish to argue with you, I have the herd to watch over.'

'My apology is heartfelt,' he let out a long breath. 'I am exhausted Imamu. I am tired of being an outcast. I just want to be given the chance to rejoin the herd. And be part of society again. I made poor choices when I was young, I know that now. I was unpleasant to you, to all of you. But I am no longer like that, I swear to the stars Imamu.'

'You weren't unpleasant Hatari.' Father turned to look directly at him.' You were appalling. You treated us all in a manner we wouldn't treat our enemies. You were nothing more than a cowardly bully. And the way you treated Talib is unforgivable.'

'It's true. And I hate myself more than any of you could hate me.' He looked down shamefully and then back into my father's eyes. 'But I am not that wildebeest any more. I have spent my sentence on the edge of this herd looking in. Watching everyone grow and move on around me. I have walked in everyone's shadow for a lifetime and I only see what I have missed. I have only known one female and sired only one son. But they too have abandoned me Imamu. I am sad that I am rejected by the herd, but I am most upset that my son doesn't respect me. That is my punishment for my life choices. That was my sentence Imamu.'

Father looked back over the herd and then towards the horizon. 'I will accept your apology for the other day. And I empathise with you, but I cannot completely forgive you after everything you have done Hatari.' He looked back at him. 'And it is not my place to forgive you on behalf of others in this herd. You need to prove to the council of elders that you have learned your lesson. Then you must prove yourself to the herd. If you want their forgiveness you need to earn it from them. The fact you have come to me and asked my forgiveness is reassuring. It takes strength to admit to ones mistakes and to seek absolution. So I will not personally deny you from rejoining this herd, so long as you are welcome by every other member. You have a lot of work ahead of you, gaining the trust of so many, but that too is part of your sentence. Only you can correct your own mistakes.'

CHASING THE RAIN

'Thank you Imamu. This means so much.' He bowed again to my father.

'Do not let the herd down Hatari. There will be no forgiveness if you wrong us again.'

Hatari said nothing. He just lowered his head once more and backed away before turning and walking along the outside of the herd. Ayana and I looked at each other but couldn't speak at first. Then she said 'your father is trusting Hatari?'

'My father is wise... He knows to keep someone like him on the right side... I trust my father's judgement. If he didn't trust Hatari, he would have told him so.' But even I was having my doubts about father's decision.

Later that day, as the sun turned bright ochre, father called a meeting for all to attend. The herd gathered round, intrigued by what father was going to announce. He was scraping some dirt from an old termite mound in front of him with his hoof. Once the excitement had died down and silence fell over the herd, father placed his front hoofs onto the mound, raising himself up to look over the sea of faces. 'I have an important announcement for you all. I have been keeping a close eye on the horizon and have some exciting news... We have been resting for a few days now and we have had a good chance to feed, and to drink plenty of water. I can now announce I have detected the signs of the long rains to the north. Tonight we can celebrate the arrival of Masika, for tomorrow we head forth and begin chasing the rains.'

The herd erupted into excitement. This was the turning point the heard have been anticipating. We have trekked for miles from the east. Now these signs father speaks of mean the storms to the north of here are about to begin. These storms bring long periods of rain, lasting for days at a time. They create the excitement within us because they mean the grasslands will be bountiful. There will be grasses and flowers, leaves on the trees for our friends the giraffe and plenty of water to wash it all down. This is the sign that brings life to our herd, and brings joy to all our hearts.

'Tonight we can be happy and celebrate the journey so far,' father continued. 'But remember, tomorrow marks the start of our next expedition. We must keep clear minds. Get plenty of rest in preparation for the journey. The rewards from this trek will be great, but we must not lose our focus. We must not become complaisant in our excitement. The journey takes us past the granite outcrops. It is fraught with danger. Ensure you remain as the herd you are. Watch out for each other and keep your young ones safe. But above all, enjoy the rewards it will bring.' The crowd erupted once again. Father lowered his head to mark the end of the meeting and then looked up and shouted 'let the celebrations begin.'

The evening was a joyous occasion. Elders were singing old songs and the adults were dancing and laughing. Even the youngsters were playing in the moonlight, the first time they had been allowed to stay up past sunset. We were once again relaxed and happy. The celebrations went long into the evening, and when we all finally led down to rest, the elders told stories about the granite pass and the green luscious meadows to the north.

3
Trekking North

It had been almost fifty days since we left the sanctity of the three lakes. The celebrations were memorable and even now it is often the topic of conversation on the long arduous walk to the north. The morning after the celebrations, the herd held a ceremony in respect of Duni. Efia couldn't face it so soon after losing her daughter the way she did and holding it on the morning of the trek north made it much more poignant. It brought everyone together and solidified our bond for the expedition we were about to embark on.

My siblings were coping far better with the distances the herd were walking each day. They enjoyed the celebrations by the lakes and were still talking about the night they stayed up past their bed time. I think it's the thought of more celebrations like that one that keeps them moving so quickly. After Duni's ceremony, Imari came and spoke to me privately. The adults were careful not to worry the youngsters with talk of attacks in case it made them too wary on the journey, but Imari said it was sad what had happened. When I asked what he meant, he told me 'Duni was taken by the monster in my dream wasn't she? She was drinking from the river and it took her.' He must have heard what had happened to her when everyone was panicking, so I just told him that Duni had an accident. I said Efia was sad, but the ceremony would make sure Duni is kept safe by the other spirits, and can watch over her mother on her journey. He couldn't understand it all at first because he said he was sure he saw her taken. He then started to cry when he said 'I should have told father about the monster.' To hear him talk like this upset me and I told him that his bad dreams were just caused by the sound of the thunder. I spent as much time with him and Karamu as I could, and all our games of Ampe seemed to help him forget about Duni, and he even seemed to be sleeping better too.

I told my father that Ayana and I had seen Hatari mixing with Thairu and his friends, and they gave this information to Idriis and Hekima. The council of elders met to discuss Hatari's sentence. The outburst marred his name and made their decision difficult, but he swore it was in support of the herd rather than an attack on the leaders. He also said that Thairu had been approaching him, and that he had told them repeatedly that he cannot speak to them due to his sentence. The elders sent him away, and he remained on the outskirts for another few days before he was once again called back to hear his fate. Idriis and Hekima pleaded with the council that he shows little to no sign of change, but they were outvoted by all of the others. Hatari is now allowed to re-enter the herd and live among us all once again. But he remains under the watchful eye of the council, and must prove to the herd that he has changed.

I spent a lot of time with Ayana after leaving the lakes, almost every day in fact. And our friendship had never been stronger. But the more I hung out with her, the more I noticed my feelings for her were changing. We talk about everything, and I know I can share my feelings with her, but whenever we get close she laughs and nudges me playfully. And every time I'm with her I seem to notice something new, something more incredible than before. She's started to develop into a beautiful young adult and I can't take my eyes off her. I find myself staring when she's talking. But if she asks if I'm ok, I just tell her I'm thinking of something else and quickly change the subject. The other day we were sitting in the sun during a rare rest stop and she placed her head on my shoulder. I could have stayed like that for the rest of the day, but unfortunately we had to move on.

I've experienced changes in myself too. Father says I am growing into adulthood quite nicely. I've had a rapid growth spurt and I'm far more muscular around my chest and shoulders. Ayana joked recently that they look broad enough to carry the entire herd. My mane has become much longer now too, as has my beard. But most noticeable of all are my horns. Over the last few weeks the small straight twigs I had growing from my head have become quite large. They've grown longer and wider and now even have a curve. They feel much heavier than before too. My parents are so happy to see my changes. Father is really proud I am turning into a strong adult, but mother keeps getting a little teary, saying how it feels like only yesterday I was her precious little child. I guess I should be really happy with the transformation I have gone through, because it means I am growing more mature. But all I can really think about is what it all brings with it. And that kind of brings me back to Ayana.

In around thirty days, I will have to make a choice that could affect my future forever. When we reach the open plains to the north, our herd will begin what we call the Rut. This is a time when all the males of our species decide if we wish to make a challenge for dominance. For myself and everyone else my age, this year marks a true rite of passage as when we take part in our first ever Rut, we become true adults.

During the rut, we choose an opponent based on whether they are stronger than us or have a much higher standing within the herd. We then carry out the display that can win or lose us our ranking. We battle our opponent using our horns, butting one another until one gives in. The entire thing looks and sounds very violent, but in reality it is merely a show of prowess, skill and elegance, hence we refer to it as a display rather than a fight. Father said I stand a good chance should I participate because my horns are already very large compared to other males my own age and ranking. He's assured me it's safe and that injury only occurs if there are mistakes. He keeps repeating that I shouldn't be so nervous which doesn't actually help, but it isn't really the display that worries me.

After the displays have taken place over the course of about six days, the females choose their suitors. Father says I won't have a problem attracting lots of females, but I can't bring myself to tell him how I really feel. Given the opportunity, I would only want to be chosen by one female, and that is Ayana. But if I decide to participate and I lose, she may not choose me at all. And if I try too hard to win, she may think I am trying to impress all the other females so I can build a harem.

During the last rut, the stronger males were approached by lots of females, and many of them chose numerous partners to build their Harems. But I would never want that, I want to follow the tradition my father chose, and Jelani too, to be chosen by a single suitor and to join through love and respect. And I would never want that with anyone other than Ayana. But if I told her any of this, of how I truly feel about her, then I could ruin any friendship we have.

Father has been showing me how to read the signs of the Serengeti, just like my grandfather did with him. He's taken me out every day to give me lessons on survival, saying it will be good to know these skills for the future. He's taught me all about the lightning, showing me how to determine if the storm on the horizon will be fruitful. How to detect the difference in colours of the grasslands in the distance to be sure they are nutritious. And he has also been telling me how to spot the signs of our enemies in the area. It has been fun to learn new skills and even the tests father has given me have been enjoyable. He has been really busy since my siblings arrived for any father-son bonding, so I look forward to each lesson he says we will have.

'Berko, Idriis has asked that I invite you to our meeting in the morning,' said father as we walked together. 'We will soon be arriving at Grumeti River and we need an extra lookout to help see the herd across safely.'

'Why has he asked for me?'

'Idriis said you were his first choice. He knows you very well, and he knows he can trust you.'

'I have a lot of respect for Idriis, but I don't think I'd be able to help for something as important as this father. I'm sorry.' My father looked disappointed by my response, 'I'm sorry if I've let you down father.'

'You have not let me down son; it takes great courage to know your own mind,' he nudged me gently. 'I love you, and it would make me proud to have you stood by my side, but the decision must be yours. I have reservations about you helping with a crossing so soon too. It is dangerous and you are only on your third journey. But you are braver than you know Berko, and very mature for your age,' he moved closer, our shoulders touching, and then he touched his cheek to mine lovingly. 'Your lessons have been going well, but you still have so much to learn. When the sun drops to the horizon, we will stop to rest, and I will teach you everything you need to know about the crossing. But the decision to help the leaders can only be yours to make Berko.' He pressed his cheek to mine again.

'Does Idriis really think I have what it takes to help?'

'He would never have asked if he did not believe in you my son. Everything happens for a reason Berko; you need to believe in your fate.'

We continued in complete silence but I needed some time to truly digest what Idriis had asked of me. So I told father I'd catch up with him and I spent a little time walking alone near the edge of the herd, not that you can ever truly be alone with all of these bodies marching along with you. Listening to the hypnotic sound of hoofs on the damp soil kept my thoughts focussed and the weight of the request started to lift off of me.

Sadly this feeling was short-lived as my thoughts soon turned to Ayana and how it could affect her if I went to help the leaders. If I agree, then I can't walk with my own family, and I want to keep them safe and Mbali too. But more importantly, I want to protect Ayana during the crossing. My siblings will be fine with both our mothers helping them across, but Ayana would be all alone.

I headed off in search of Ayana to confide in her about the crossing. I found her in the crowd and asked if she'd like to walk with me for a while. She looked really happy, 'hey Berko. I've missed you today.'

'Can we go and speak more privately?' she nudged me and smiled, then we walked towards the edge of the herd to avoid others hearing what I said.

When I told her all about the crossing she looked at me with a stunned expression.

'I knew it was a bad idea,' I said through her silence, 'I just needed a different perspective, but I guess I need to tell my father I can't do it.'

'Different perspective? You didn't even let me answer you,' she nudged me again like she always does. 'You have to do it Berko. Idriis wouldn't have asked if he didn't have a good reason,'

'But what if I mess things up for the leaders? Even being an extra lookout is a huge responsibility.'

'You're so funny Berko,' she said and then laughed softly and shook her head. 'I knew you were destined for great things. I've always known it. You have an amazing spirit, even without the gifts of the spiritualist elders it's plain to see. You are strong can't you see that? And I don't just mean physically, although you have definitely matured. I mean mentally. You put everyone else before yourself. You help your family. You look after your siblings when they're too much for your mother. You always help me. You're great Berko, and Idriis can obviously see that too.'

'Great? None of that stuff makes me great Ayana. I'm not the only one who helps their parents or their friends.'

'That day you saved my life; you didn't think about it, you just stepped in and risked your own life for me. You've always been amazing. You possess all of the same qualities as the leaders of this herd. Well... all except one,' she smiled and walked ahead.

'And what's that?' I asked, trying to catch up with her.

'Self belief Berko! If you had any real confidence in yourself, you'd know that what I see in you is the same as everyone else sees. A strong, smart and modest wildebeest. You have all of the qualities of the strongest leaders of this herd. You're intelligent, selfless and you have integrity. You're courageous, but you don't even realise it,' she let me catch up and walk beside her again. 'And all of those qualities are what make me like you so much.'

'So you really think I should do it. I should help the herd across the river?'

'Yes,' she nudged me again. 'I'd feel much safer if you were there helping us. And Idriis wouldn't have asked if he didn't have trust in you.'

I thought about everything and continued on beside her in complete silence. And every time I thought of another excuse not to do it, she just looked at me and I knew not to even speak.

On my way to find father, the sky turned dark as thick grey clouds rolled in off the mountains. Rain started to fall. I spotted him and cantered over through the downpour. We stood at the edge of the herd to start my lesson. The rain got heavier and wind blasted across the plain, blowing the raindrops straight at us. We turned to face away from it to avoid it hitting our faces and father looked wary, so I asked if he was ok.

'I am just hoping this rain doesn't continue for long. I do not want any setbacks for our crossing,' he replied.

'I'll be sure to keep a close eye on the current father, before I allow anyone to enter the water.'

Father looked up at me through the heavy rain, squinting as the droplets ran from his brow. 'Does this mean you are going to join me at the front Berko?'

'I have thought long and hard about everything. And you are right, I should believe in my fate. Besides, there are certain wildebeests relying on me. I can't let them down,' I smiled.

'I didn't want you to feel pressured Berko, and I will admit I am still a little wary of you joining us for this at your age, but I am also happy you have made your decision. It shows Idriis' judgement in your maturity was not misplaced,' he smiled back at me. 'So... let's begin your lesson.'

He dragged his hoof through the mud to create a long, curved groove and told me to wait. We looked over the herd and watched the others enjoying the rain. They were jumping and frolicking, letting the droplets wash their coats and they were stretching out their legs to relax their aching muscles. Father looked back and pointed to the groove he'd just made in the mud, now filled by the rain. 'Water! It brings life. But it can easily take it away if not respected,' he said dipping his hoof in the puddle he'd formed. 'This line represents the river Berko, it will be deep and treacherous. It will be down to us and the other leaders to walk the bank in the morning and find a safe place to enter. An area like this would be most suitable,' he pointed at a wide section by the curve, 'because the current will be weaker and the water shallow. We will try to find a low section of bank that allows us all to enter the water easily. Once we are satisfied, we can call the herd to join us. Only when many bodies are lining the bank, will we lead them across; because once we begin we cannot turn back. Some of the leaders will enter and make the crossing ahead of the herd, and then those of us on this side will guide the rest. We need to be vigilant whichever our role. And we need to communicate at all times. I will teach you the signals we all use later.'

'That doesn't sound as scary as I first thought.'

'That is merely the start of it Berko. It is not only the water that can take our lives. There are our enemies too. The water conceals many of our foes. Firstly there are the crocodiles, and you have seen for yourself what they can do. They are cunning, able to hide out of view. Even if we are observant, it is still possible to miss them. Secondly there are the hippos. They are large animals Berko; their mouths could easily fit around your body.'

'Do they eat us Father?' I asked, with a shake in my throat.

'No. They are like us, they feed on the plants. But they have killed our kind before. You need to be wary if they have young with them. The adults are twice the size of you. If they are alone, then they should cause us no harm. There are no other enemies within the waters for you to fear.' I sighed playfully. 'But remember Berko, water brings vegetation. The banks are often lined with tall grasses and reeds. These provide hiding places for our other enemies, the lions, hyenas, cheetahs and even leopards. I have experienced the ambush of a leopard and survived thanks only to Kwame, but it is rare to be that lucky. They are all clever hunters and will do anything to catch one of us. Keep a close eye on the banks, and watch for unusual movement within the reeds. This is a lot to take in son, but I know you will make me proud.' The rain stopped and we both shook to remove the water from our coats. 'A positive sign from the spirits,' said father as he looked over at the breaks in the clouds where red light of the setting sun was shining through with so much promise. Father ran through the signals the leaders use to communicate during the crossings and then went over everything again to make sure I understood it all. Standing with him as he entrusted me with this sort of information gave me a feeling of pride, but I couldn't shake the nervous ache I had growing in my stomach. I was starting to understand why this is usually kept from us until we are on our fifth journey; everyone might say I am mature, but the talk of all our enemies is terrifying; I don't think I'll get any sleep tonight after this lesson.

The warmth of the rising sun on my face and the red glow though my eyelids was enough to wake me from my light sleep. The morning mist was burning off and the sky was clearing quickly. I guess it was a perfect day to cross a river.

I was full of apprehension for the day ahead, but also strangely excited to be joining the leaders on the river survey. I was awake before my siblings so I ate my breakfast quietly. Mother kissed me on the cheek and wished me luck, and then she turned to father and said quietly 'you will keep a close eye on him won't you Imamu?'

'Of course my love, but he will be fine. It is no different than making the crossing with the rest of the herd,' he kissed her on the cheek and we both walked away to meet Jelani.

Ayana quietly wished me luck as I set off with father and Jelani to meet the others. Talib and Kwame were waiting near some large rocks with Idriis and Hekima. Talib touched his cheek to mine and said quietly, 'I am truly proud to see you here Berko.'

We waited for the other leaders from the zebra and eland troops and then Afia came over and said to father 'so he is finally joining us Imamu? It's good to see you here Berko.'

'Thanks. You knew I would join you?'

'Idriis has been discussing it for a while. Especially after your bravery by the water recently,' she said.

'I can't show my gratitude enough Berko. Without you, my Ayana would not be here. Thank you once again,' said Jelani and he pressed his cheek against mine.

I didn't know what to say so I just stood there and felt my face getting warmer with embarrassment. When the others arrived from the other side of the herd, they all welcomed me to the group, saying they were happy to see me here. My father looked at me and winked and then he looked to the others and said 'enough about Berko, his head will be swelling. We must go to the river and make our plans.' I thanked him quietly when we were all walking away and he gave me a reassuring smile and nudged me playfully.

When we got close to the river, the leaders all started to spread out. Father told me to stick with him so he could show me what to do. We walked towards the riverbank and each leader signalled to the next to indicate they were stopping.

Father and I stopped at a spot that was clear of any grass or reeds, but the water level was pretty low and the riverbank was like a sheer cliff, the herd would never be able to climb down. But although it wasn't great for crossing, the bank gave us a good vantage point to look right down stream. The water was calm and clear of enemies.

'Many of the animals, particularly our enemies are probably down within the vast lake,' whispered father. 'They will be taking advantage of the animals being drawn to it to drink. I have a positive feeling about our crossing.'

We all reconvened and Talib told us he'd found an ideal spot for crossing, 'the banks are quite high, but they are not as steep as up here, I think it is our best option if we are to cross today,' he said.

We all followed him and the other leaders scanned it for the best means of access and to check the lie of the bank.

Talib and Afia stood guard at the crossing point to indicate where the herd should gather. The rest of us went back and rounded everyone up. Father, Jelani and Mirembe from the zebra troop called the meeting and the herd started to approach slowly. Father reported it was time to leave and they followed us tentatively towards the river.

I spotted Ayana in the crowd with both our mothers and my siblings. She smiled at me and bowed her head as if to make light of me being stood at the front of the herd. As we walked, an ache of nausea churned in my stomach as reality hit me. And the weight of responsibility was falling on top of me like rocks from the cliffs.

At the river, the leaders and I stood on the bank and waited for the mass of bodies to build up behind us. We were watching all the time for movement in the water or anything in the long grass on the other bank. We were careful not to make any noise when we were surveying it and the herd knew to do the same. There was a deafening silence over the plain as the dark mass of animals grew larger and packed tightly together.

Talib and Afia had waited until we got there and once the time had come to start the crossing, they and Mirembe made the first move. They dropped over the edge of the bank, disappearing from view. And as the herd edged ever closer, Talib moved carefully into the water, feeling the riverbed to make sure it wasn't too deep for the smaller among us. Afia was checking the current wasn't too strong, but being so small and light had to fight the gentle swell.

When he was half way across, Talib turned his head and signalled to the other leaders it was safe. The atmosphere was tense; members of the herd were wrestling with themselves, all trying to push forwards to make the first move, but their legs weren't allowing them. As the others behind were nudging forward and jostling for position, the animals at the front had no choice but to go. They dropped over the edge of the bank and tried to enter the water cautiously, but some of the animals still on the bank couldn't stop themselves and were pushed by their instincts. They jumped over the heads of the front row and straight into the water. The splash caused a rush of fear and excitement through the herd and they all started to push forward as one. Father started to call out, urging the herd to move and cross as quickly as they could. The crossing had officially started and there was no stopping it now.

The water was being churned and mixed, and the muddy foam on the surface was being swirled into spirals with every splash of a hoof. The splashing was deafening and the water sprayed high into the air, right over the heads of the animals making the crossing. All the different animals were marching across together. The adults were helping the youngsters to swim through the deep water. It was exhilarating and it was also terrifying.

By now some of the animals were already on the other bank, shaking water from their coats and seeking space on the plains to rest their aching legs and dry off in the morning sun. Looking back down the plain, the herd went on for what looked like miles. It was difficult to tell how we'd all get to the other side. Among the blur of faces I saw Ayana clearly, then I saw my family and Mbali.

I scanned the water thoroughly for danger and looked down over the bank to make sure it was safe for my siblings to enter. My sister called out to me excitedly, like she hadn't seen me in ages, and when I smiled and nodded at her, she giggled with glee. Imari was staring at me and smiling, holding his head up as high as he could. I watched as they made their crossing, occasionally glancing up and down the river to double check it was safe.

When they reached the other bank, Ayana helped my mother out of the water and then they all scooped my siblings out and ushered them up the steep bank. At the top, Karamu and Imari both looked back at me, so I threw them another nod and they both ran off giggling again.

The sun was almost directly above us when the final members of the herd reached us. Father raised his head straight back to signal to Jelani and Kwame that it was soon time to make the crossing ourselves and they responded by dipping their heads sideways, which father reminded me meant they understood his message. We scanned the bank on our side and watched the plain for signs of our enemies who could have followed us, waiting to attack anyone trailing the herd. When we were sure it was safe, we joined the others and followed them into the water.

The cold water shocked my body after being in the sun for so long, my muscles tightened and I took a sharp inward breath. The current was strong beneath the surface and the water was deeper than it looked from above, so we had to swim the middle section.

Ahead of me, an older wildebeest was struggling to fight the fast flow of the water and was panicking. I swam up beside him and pushed my shoulder under his front leg to keep him afloat. As the water became shallower, the riverbed came into contact with the bottom of my hoofs, and the older wildebeest wearily walked out of the water before he thanked me for assisting him. I gave him a helpful shove so he could get up the bank and he walked gingerly over to the herd.

Father came out of the water and we both walked up the bank together. We looked back to check there were no stragglers in the river before shaking the water from our coats. The other leaders came over and congratulated me for doing well before going off into the herd to find their families.

'I am very proud of you my son,' said father. 'That was a true act of kindness you showed. You definitely proved yourself today, well done.' He touched his cheek to mine. As we headed back towards the herd, he kept looking at me and smiling. It gave me a real sense of pride to be there with my father.

Our crossing was truly rewarded. In the bright, hot sunshine, luscious open grasslands spread out in front of us and stretched all the way to the horizon. The rains had provided enough grass and vegetation for us all and we took full advantage. We all took a much needed rest before spreading out and feeding wherever we wished. There was a wonderful energy over the herd and we stayed in the grasslands right through to morning.

The following day, before the sun had even woken up, everyone fed in readiness for the walk towards the woodlands. I had breakfast with Ayana and told her all about my experience of the crossing. I told her how my siblings were acting when I got back, 'they were giggling and excited, like they hadn't seen me in days.'

'They were talking about you the whole time, they're just proud to have such a famous brother,' she said.

'What do you mean?'

'Well, their brother, a leader of the herd on his third journey. It's quite impressive Berko.'

'What? But I was only helping. They said they needed an extra look out Ayana.'

'Are you really that naive Berko? It was Grumeti River. The same place Talib proved his worthiness as a leader. What do you think all of your lessons have been for? You don't see anyone else being taught the skills of the Serengeti. I think it's great.'

'We have all started our lessons. Your father has been teaching you about the herd too.'

'Yes, but I'm learning about the dangers and the route. You are being taught everything. My father said you are showing real promise.'

'I think I'd be the first to know if I was being taught to be a leader Ayana,' I laughed and she just shrugged and went back to her breakfast.

When we went back to our families, my father said he wanted me to join him later for the leaders meeting. And after my talk with Ayana, that same feeling of nausea I had before the crossing returned with a vengeance.

I took my siblings to some open plains to give my parents a break and we played a game of Ampe, but Imari tired of it quickly. He wanted to ask me all about the river and then Karamu soon lost interest in the game too and pressed me for answers.

'So? Is it fun being in charge Berko? Do you get treated different by the adults? Do you get to talk to all the leaders? Do you get any treats Berko?'

'Take a breath Karamu, you'll pass out.' I said, before getting them both to sit with me on the grass. 'The crossing was ok.'

'Only ok?' said Imari screwing up his face with disappointment.

'Yes, it went smoothly. There were no problems and everyone got across safely.'

'Boring!' he said sarcastically, rolling his eyes.

'Yeah, but what's it like to be in charge?' asked Karamu excitedly.

'I'm not actually in char...' I paused as I thought about what Ayana said at breakfast. Then I saw the disappointment on Karamu's face, so I leant in closer and said quietly, 'It was scary, I had to go right up to the river and check if there was anything that could *jump out!*' I leapt forward and they both screamed and fell backwards onto the grass giggling. 'Then I had to listen out for any *roars!*' they screamed again and giggled even louder than before. Then they looked up at me smiling, their eyes widening with anticipation. I tried to think of something else to say, to keep them amused.

'*Roar!*' Ayana called behind me and stepped lightly on my tail, making me jump forward onto Karamu who laughed uncontrollably. 'Sorry Berko, I couldn't resist,' Ayana said and she laughed, and Imari and Karamu both giggled with her. 'I told your mother I'd look after these two terrors for a while,' Imari screwed his face up at Ayana playfully. 'Your father said it's almost time for your meeting. Better get to it oh mighty leader.'

'Thanks Ayana... Okay, I'll see you all later,' I was trying not to look at any of them. I ran off quickly into the herd to hide my warm face and my embarrassment of being so easily scared, and I went in search of my father.

The meeting was pretty boring to start with; everyone was just talking about the crossing and the weather to the north. They all said how impressed they were with me yesterday, but I didn't really feel I'd done that much to get all this praise, so I just smiled and thanked them politely. While they were speaking about the upcoming days, I felt left out, so I just had to stand there and listen. My mind started to wander to my conversation with Ayana this morning and I glazed over, but then Talib spoke directly to me, taking me by complete surprise. 'You made quite an impression yesterday Berko. The herd were as impressed as we were at your performance. You were the subject of many of the conversations I heard.'

'Really?' I blushed and my voice cracked. 'They were impressed by me?'

'Of course, why would they not be?' he took a deep breath. 'But there is something else I need to tell you,' he said coming closer to me. 'I overheard some gossip between a group of wildebeest, about two years older than you. One of them was telling the rest of the group that they had heard you were trying to get yourself noticed by all of the leaders, and you would do anything to impress us, even push your friends aside. I put her straight of course, but when I questioned her about it, she insisted she had heard it from an adult.'

'Do you know who told her this?' asked father.

'Hatari, who else?' Talib sighed. 'I even caught him telling someone else when I went to question him. He said it is unfair that Berko should be helping on only his third journey when everyone else must wait until their fifth,' he turned to look back at me. 'But we all agree you were well suited to the role yesterday Berko, that is why Idriis asked for your help. And I was really impressed by what I saw,' he touched his forehead to mine as reassurance.

'I really don't like Hatari, but maybe he's right,' I said. 'And even if he didn't start these rumours, I'm sure there were many already thinking it.'

'There will always be those among the herd that do not agree with the decisions of the leaders Berko. Usually it is a little jealousy,' said Kwame.

Idriis stepped forward and touched my cheek, 'Berko, I am sorry I was not completely truthful with you. I wanted to confirm what I already knew. But this was a test. I could not tell you. It would have affected how you acted during the crossing. And that could have clouded your judgement during such a critical time...' he came closer to me. 'I see something in you that I have not seen in any of the older animals. I have watched every member of this herd closely, and you have always stood out. You have a strong spirit Berko, the likes of which I have never seen before,' he touched his forehead to mine. 'Hatari's views hold little validity among any of us, and it would upset me to think his words would make you question yourself like this,' he sighed heavily.

'I am sorry if I caused upset Berko,' added Talib. 'I wouldn't have said anything if I had known it would do that, but with the rut fast approaching for you all, I thought it best to mention it.'

'You were right to bring this up Talib,' said father. 'We should all be vigilant of Hatari at the moment.'

'Why does the rut matter?' I asked.

'It is the time our standing within the herd is challenged,' said father. 'If others realise you were being tested at the Grumeti, then you could become a target. I am so sorry my son, this is all my fault. I should never have pushed for this right before the rut. I didn't think.'

'You didn't push this father. It was my decision to actually help you. And besides, I still haven't decided if I want to participate in the rut this season.'

'I am so sorry Berko,' said Idriis. 'In my haste to ask you to help at the crossing, I may have already made that decision for you. If others think you are being considered a potential leader, then you will be a viable opponent. And if they can beat you during a display, they will see that as an invitation to challenge a leader of this herd. I really am sorry Berko.'

I thought for a while as this all sank in. 'Well everyone knows I am the son of Imamu, so I was likely to be challenged because of that anyway. I guess that just helps with my decision,' I said flippantly. 'And as you always say father, if it is written in my stars then who am I to stand in the way of fate?' I smiled and shrugged. 'I will just have to face it when the time comes.'

'I am so proud of you Berko,' said father.

'You have raised an amazing son Imamu,' said Talib and he touched his forehead to mine again. 'I would be very proud to have a son like you Berko. Very proud indeed.'

'You have an incredible spirit Berko,' said Idriis. 'You have matured quickly, and yesterday you truly proved yourself. If you can follow your spirit, then one day I could see you working alongside all of us.'

They all touched their cheeks to mine and I felt my face getting warm with embarrassment again. And I guess Ayana was right after all; I really have been naive.

That evening I sat alone in the long grass watching the stars sparkling above me like the sun on the water's surface. The woodlands are only a day's trek away and when we pass through to the sacred plains beyond, I will have to be prepared for the Rut. I really didn't want to take part in it, but I couldn't tell father I wasn't really ok with that. He'd feel too guilty. What I said to him was true, I was expecting to be challenged because I'm his son, but I wouldn't have cared if I lost. I don't have anything to prove. But after everything the leaders said, it's completely different. I could be a target by anyone, so I guess I need to be prepared. And I really need to think long and hard about protecting myself.

'Hey, I've been searching everywhere for you.'

'Oh hi Ayana. Sorry I just needed some space for a while.'

'Is everything ok Berko?'

'I just have a lot on my mind,' I looked directly at her and immediately felt much more relaxed. 'You were right of course, Idriis was testing me. He said I had a strong spirit. Really strong, apparently. But because of the test I may be a target by some of the others during the rut. I wasn't even going to participate, and now I might not have a choice.'

'Are you crazy Berko? You have to take part in the rut this year.'

'But I didn't think you would want me to. You've always said the rut is full of arrogant males trying to look good for the females. I've never been the type to show off. You know that.'

'Yes but this year's different,' she looked down at the ground and kicked the grass lightly. 'I mean, you have been told your spirit is strong,' she looked back up at me. 'So you'll have fate on your side. You'll be fine. Besides, you're not arrogant Berko. You're the most modest I know. Plus it is a tradition after all,' she nudged me playfully.

'It's still terrifying, even if it is just a display... but I suppose I could ask my father for some guidance. You know, just in case.'

'You'll do well. The girls will be lining up to meet you.'

'Ha, yeah right.'

'It's true. I even heard Zuri and her friends talking about you today.'

'Really? Zuri? Wow, she never speaks to me. I'm surprised she even knows my name.'

'Yeah... well... you'll be able to get closer to her if you win then Berko. And all her popular friends too,' she said abruptly. She looked back towards the herd. 'I think I can hear my mother calling me. I have to go.' She turned and walked away quickly.

'I didn't hear your m... Wait... Ayana... is everything OK?' But she didn't turn back to answer.

Over breakfast I couldn't stop thinking about Ayana's reaction last night, so I rushed my grass and headed off to find her. Mbali told me she'd gone to have breakfast with a friend so I searched all over to see if I could spot them, but she was nowhere to be seen. Before I could finish searching for her, my father called out to me and the herd were preparing to move out.

Father and I walked at the front of the herd and talked about the upcoming Rut. I asked him what I needed to do and he said he'd teach me the tactics and the skills I'd need at the next rest stop. On the journey he was telling me about some of his past fights and how he's learned to outsmart his opponents. 'It's all about skill Berko. Strength is always secondary in the rut. Just look at Jelani.'

CHASING THE RAIN

'I heard that!' Jelani called as he walked over to us. 'So you are thinking of taking part after all Berko? I will have to teach you some of my moves. Don't listen to your father. He is awful compared to me.' He nudged father to the side and laughed.

'When we stop shortly we will both teach you,' said father. 'We'll let you decide who is worst... I mean best,' and they both laughed.

'Thank you,' I said and I smiled proudly. I walked beside them for a while, listening to them talk about their past experiences of the Rut and I found their stories fascinating. But I still couldn't get the thought of last night out of my head. Had I somehow upset Ayana? We were getting on as we always do, and then she just changed. For no reason.

I kept looking back across the herd to try to spot Ayana. If I could find her, then I could check she is ok. I spotted my family and then I could see Mbali talking with my mother, but I couldn't see Ayana anywhere.

When we stopped to rest, Ayana didn't come over to eat with her parents. I wanted to go and search for her but then father nudged me, 'are you ready for your lesson son? Remember, we will let you decide who is best,' and he winked as Jelani was coming over to join us.

They both showed me different ways to outsmart your opponent and taught me how to read the others next move. After a few rounds of practicing, they asked me to try.

First I faced my father who taught me how to use my weight to bring my horns down on top of my opponents head, causing them to lose their balance.

After a few attempts I was really starting to get the hang of it.

I then faced Jelani. He showed me how to display one way then quickly change direction to come in from the opposite side to confuse the opponent and catch them unaware. We practiced for a while and then I fought father again. I was starting to really enjoy it and then Jelani said he would show me another move.

'You are becoming an expert already Berko. You will be unstoppable.' Jelani shouted as he brought his horns down.

I spotted Ayana from the corner of my eye, and distracted, I turned my head to the side to look at her. The base of Jelani's horns caught me on the side of the face and I went crashing into the dirt, dazed and shaken. My father ran over to me and helped me up, asking if I was ok and Jelani kept apologising to me and father for hitting me, but I said I was fine. By the time I got back to my hoofs and shook the dust and dizziness off, Ayana had disappeared. She'd walked back into the herd and out of sight once again.

It'd been two days since my lesson with Jelani and my father, and I still hadn't seen Ayana. I'd tried repeatedly to catch up with her, but she always had somewhere to be and when I went to find her, Mbali would tell me she'd left in a hurry. The rut was starting soon and I wanted to speak to her before it began, just to find out what I did to upset her.

CHASING THE RAIN

I asked Mbali again if she knew what was wrong with Ayana or where she was. She told me Ayana had promised to watch Imari and Karamu later so I might have a good chance of seeing her then.

I took my siblings to the meadow to play Ampe with them. I knew Ayana would never go against her promise to an adult and would come to play with them both. When I saw her coming I told my siblings to carry on playing without me. 'Ayana, I've missed you lately. Where have you been going?'

'I've been spending time with some friends. But I wouldn't expect you to care Berko.'

'What do you mean?'

'I saw you practicing with my father. For someone who isn't bothered about the Rut, you took it pretty seriously. Look at the bump on your face.'

'I don't get you Ayana. It was you who said I should take part. Our fathers were just preparing me in case I'm challenged.'

'Well you stand a good chance of impressing Zuri and her friends now,' she said before turning and walking away.

'Ayana wait...' I ran ahead and stopped her. 'Do you really think I'd want to impress Zuri? I don't even like her, or her friends. They always follow the older males around, and talk about themselves all the time. Like I said, I was surprised they even knew my name. Zuri used to pick on me when we were in the nursery group and once she even kicked dust in my face when I stuck up for you...' I stopped speaking abruptly.

'You stuck up for me?' She started to smile a little.

'Yes... They were going to push you in the lake when the parents weren't watching. I said I'd push them in first if they even tried it.'

'I can't believe you've never told me that before,'

'I was protecting you Ayana. I didn't want you to think Zuri or her friends disliked you.'

'I'm sorry I've been avoiding you Berko... It's just... when I told you Zuri was talking about you; you seemed excited at the idea. And then I saw you practicing with my father,' she touched her cheek to mine. 'I guess I was just preparing myself early for the inevitable. I mean, after the rut we probably won't get to hang out any more.'

'I would never want to take part if it meant losing you Ayana.'

She smiled and turned away from me quickly, 'Karamu! I think its Berko's turn to be *it*,' and she ran over to my siblings to join in their game.

When the herd set off for the north again, Ayana and I walked with my siblings. Karamu kept boasting about winning the game and dancing around Imari. He was getting more and more annoyed and asked if I'd tell her off. 'Sorry Imari, you've taught her too well.' Ayana nudged me and giggled as Imari huffed and screwed up his face at me.

The woodlands were coming into view in the distance and there were brown shapes dancing through the trees. 'Imari, Karamu, look over there.'

'Who are they?' they both said with excitement.

'They're our good friends the baboons. They always give us the best reception when we reach the woodlands. They should have had their babies by now so you will get to meet them too. And I'm pretty sure they will be really happy to meet you.'

'I can't wait,' said Karamu joyfully and she and Imari ran off to find my mother and tell her the exciting news.

Ayana walked closely beside me, 'are you ok Berko?' she asked.

'I think so... It's just seeing the baboons. It means we're getting closer to the woodlands. And just beyond are the sacred plains. I just don't know if I'm ready to be challenged.'

4

The Annual Rut

On the open plains the Rut was in full swing. The sound of horns crashing together was echoing through the herd like thunder. So far I've been lucky to just observe it all and haven't been challenged despite now being more of a target. And I don't have any interest in challenging anyone as I have nothing to prove. So I am just enjoying the spectacle from afar.

The Rut is only carried out by the males, and it's the males who also keep more of an eye on proceedings, despite it being our way of *impressing* the females. We watch to see how the others are doing and any male wishing to join the rut will challenge another based on what they've seen or how their ranking has increased. The whole thing feels like a celebration because it helps us keep our ancient traditions alive as well as build new friendships along the way.

I'd been watching a great display between a highly experienced elder and a young strong male hoping for a greater challenge. Their Rut lasted for ages and although they looked like they were trying to kill each other, they were both laughing the whole time. I was really enjoying the festival and I was starting to feel more relaxed. But then Talib came to speak to me and told me he'd heard Hatari was vying for position. He's been walking around with his group of adolescents challenging younger wildebeest. Talib told me to keep a look out because he was looking to fight young males with significant standings. 'He might challenge you because your ranking is now closer to the leaders. So just be careful Berko, I don't want you getting hurt by someone like him.'

The following day Hatari came over to where I was feeding and his group of adolescents stood around him. One of his followers approached me, 'Hatari would like to speak to you,' he said sharply.

'I'm not interested.'

'Hatari doesn't care if you are interested or not. He would like to speak to you. If you are supposed to be a leader, you can't be a coward.'

'I'm not a coward. I just don't think enough of Hatari to stop my lunch.'

'If you choose to back down before you have even been challenged then you will never have the respect of the herd.'

'Challenged? I thought he only wanted to speak?' He stood silently staring back at me. 'Look, I don't care. Hatari is past it,' I continued. 'He lost the respect of this herd long before we were even born. If challenging first timers is his plan to gain admiration, then he might as well give up now. And if he needs to send you in to face his opponent for him, then I really don't see him as much of a threat.' I knew Hatari had already beaten several other males and was beginning to build his ranking, but I hoped he would back down if I didn't bite.

'Look coward! If you want us all to go and announce that you bowed out to Hatari, then we will. The word will spread pretty quickly to the rest of the males that you forfeited your Rut and you will soon lose their respect. And if you think Hatari is a loser, imagine what others would think of you for backing down...' he paused, realising what he'd just said. He turned quickly to look at Hatari. 'Sorry Sir. I didn't mean...'

'Fine, I'll accept his challenge. Even if he doesn't have the courage to speak to me himself,' I looked over to Hatari who was standing beside some rocks. 'I will face you later today Hatari, when the sun begins to lower.'

He raised his head slowly to acknowledge me and let me know he both understood and agreed with what I'd said. His accomplice went back to join the others and Hatari kicked him in the shin for his earlier comment. They all walked off together, with Hatari leading them.

Hearing my conversation, father came over and warned me against fighting Hatari. 'You have nothing to prove Berko, and nothing to gain from fighting him. I don't trust Hatari; he is not one to follow the rules,' he said.

'Its fine father, I know too well he can be under-hoofed. I'm prepared for his tactics and I think I can outsmart him.' But I didn't expect Hatari to fight fairly against me, the son of his longest foe.

I told father I needed some time to collect my thoughts and went to find some fresh lush grass to fill my stomach before my battle. Hatari is much weaker than I am, but I don't trust this to be an easy display. So I need the energy to face him; if not for my muscles then for my mind.

I tried to spend time on my own until I faced Hatari to keep my mind focused, but other wildebeest kept coming over to wish me luck. There were even some I'd never met who wanted to see me beat Hatari. Then a young male came over, 'Berko?' He asked with a weakness in his voice.

'Yes?' I looked up and saw him standing ahead of me. He limped up to me, he was covered in blood. 'Are you ok?' I asked, heading over to help him sit down.

'Thank you. Yes I am ok. My name is Nemsi, I have come to warn you against facing Hatari. All the males are speaking of your fight later today, and how they want you to defeat him. But he is not a worthy opponent. He does not fight with honour. He does not follow the rules. He selected me because I am also the son of a leader. My father is Oman.'

'I've met him.'

'Yes, he speaks fondly of you Berko,' he looked up at me. 'But this is what Hatari is capable of.' He showed me the injuries he'd sustained. 'He didn't follow the rules of our ancestors. He chose to fight for his place in the herd. He used tactics that are not in the spirit of the display. And he fought with the help of others.'

'His followers? He can't have help to carry out a display.'

'They stood around me so I could not display. I tried to take my turn but they prevented me. And when he took his turn, they moved in and pushed me to the ground. They held me down. I felt humiliated. But that was not enough for Hatari. These injuries you see were not caused during the display, but after. When I was already on the ground. He told me to tell anyone who asked that they were from the fight, and if I didn't, he'd come back and finish the job properly.'

'Didn't anybody step in to help?'

'We were alone. He said he wanted to do the display away from the herd. I didn't want to be seen losing my first ever fight so I followed him to the open plain. I was foolish.' He tried to stand but had to sit again. 'But you don't have to be Berko. You can forfeit and protect yourself.'

'I can't...'

'Don't be foolish Berko.' He shouted, cutting me off. 'Look at what he and his gang did to me. I too am the son of a leader, and I have yet to prove myself. But that didn't stop Hatari.' He lowered his voice. 'In you he sees a real opportunity. He thinks you are an easy opponent and a fast step up to leadership. If he does to you what he did to me, then this herd could be doomed.' He forced himself to his feet, grimacing through the pain. 'Please give it real thought Berko. You don't have anything to prove to this herd. But you have lots to lose. Hatari needs to be stopped, but you are not ready to do that. If you tell your father, he could stop him.' He turned and started to limp away.

'Thank you Nemsi,' I called out. 'I will give it some thought.' But I couldn't forfeit. This could be my best chance to show Hatari's true colours to the rest of the herd. If I could display with him in the open plains, and prove he disrespects our ancient traditions, then the council would see he hasn't changed. And he would have to be exiled once and for all.

I stood alone again with just my thoughts. Watching as my shadow moved directly beneath me, I knew it was time to finally find Hatari. As I walked through the herd, the other males were wishing me luck, pressing their cheeks to mine in support and telling me to show him who's in charge. It gave me a much needed burst of energy to know I had the support from so many wildebeest.

I found Hatari; his gang of adolescents were huddled around him. Two were rubbing his shoulders with their horns and the others were giving him tips on how to fight me.

'Hatari, are you ready to face me?' I called loudly. I could feel the adrenaline surging through my body.

He turned and started towards me at a slow pace with his gang backing him up. 'Thought you had backed out Berko,' he said arrogantly. 'I thought you were too cowardly to face me.'

'That's rich coming from you Hatari. At least I'm not scared to face you alone.'

'My boys are simply here to learn. Nothing more.'

'Well I hope you are all getting a good lesson in how to be gutless.' Hatari lunged forward at me. 'Ok so shall we start Hatari?'

'I thought we could find somewhere a bit less overlooked. I am looking forward to beating you Berko, but I am not that evil. I don't want to completely humiliate you in front of the herd,' he looked back at his gang and they all smiled at him. 'I thought we could go to the open plains.'

'I can be gracious in defeat Hatari, I'm happy to face you here whatever the outcome.'

He looked back at his gang again.

'Well, if we go to that outcrop, we could all watch from the top Sir,' said Shomari, one of the gang. The others all agreed enthusiastically.

'Fine,' I said, 'As long as you only watch. And the result needs to be told correctly to the herd on our return. You can't gain points through lying.'

'Agreed,' said Hatari, and he led the way towards the outcrop.

We headed away from the herd and into the open plains. My heart was pounding and my mouth was as dry as the savannah. I was scanning left and right to spot my father or one of the other leaders, but I couldn't see them. Everyone was too involved in the Rut to notice us walking so far away from the herd. And the further we went, the more wary I became. I should have listened to Nemsi. And I should have told my father what Hatari had done to him.

Thairu and Shomari approached the small outcrop but they didn't slow down. They just continued to walk with true determination. 'I think this is as good a place as any Hatari, the herd won't see you lose out here,' I said trying to disguise my nerves.

'Nice try Berko, but we didn't mean here,' the gang all laughed. 'We are heading there,' he said gesturing towards the woodlands. Ahead of us was a huge tower of granite, like the giant hoof of a zebra sticking out of the earth. A large circular wall of solid rock, with an opening in the nearest face; it was menacing, even from here. Waruhiu and the others ushered me on, determined not to allow me to turn back.

As we headed towards the opening, I looked back towards the herd, but they were so far away now I couldn't make out a single animal from the mass of black scattered across the plain. Occasionally the sound of crashing horns echoed across the earth like the heavy thump of my heart within my chest. I was so far from the herd now, they would never hear if I called out to them.

'After you,' said Thairu gesturing towards the opening in the rock.

'Um... thanks,' I said and walked through tentatively.

I looked up and traced the rocky walls all the way around. They were sheer with no way to climb them. The only way out was the way we'd just come in. I was trapped.

They all filed in through the opening and started to walk around me; all apart from one. Waruhiu stood at the opening, blocking my exit. Hatari stopped and stood in front of me and all of the others lined up behind me. I glanced back to my left and then my right, making sure they didn't make any sudden moves.

Hatari stepped forward. 'I will let you have the first hit Berko. Show I am playing fairly.'

'Fairly? You have me cornered. Away from the entire herd. There is nothing fair about this Rut.' I glanced to my left and right again and took a small step forward. 'I won't start until your minions are safely out of reach Hatari.'

'They are here to watch and to learn. Nothing else. I want to prove to you I am stronger. And that you are out of your depth Berko,' he stepped forward again to close the gap between us. 'Now make your move!'

I took a deep breath and bedded my back hoofs into the dust. I reared up onto my hind legs ready to bring my horns down onto the top of his head. As I stretched back Hatari butted me in the ribs, forcing me backwards. As I stumbled, Thairu tripped me with his hoof and I fell to the ground. 'Dirty tactics don't win these Ruts Hatari!' I said, quickly rolling to the left.

I got back to my feet, leaping away as Hatari charged at me. He skidded in the dirt and fell into Shomari and Thairu. They caught him and helped to stable him.

'Cowardice!' he cried. 'Dodging an advance shows you are weak Berko. You are not cut out to lead this herd.'

'That wasn't an advance, it was an attack. And it was out of turn. That is the only cowardice here. You make a mockery of our ancient practices.'

He puffed his chest and blasted air from his nostrils. He made a gesture towards Thairu and then charged at me once more. As he reached me I lowered my chin and raised my head, driving the body of my horns onto his muzzle with a loud, dull thud. He lost his balance and skidded onto his knees in the dust, dazed and shaken.

Thairu came charging towards me in retaliation for his master and I turned to my left and thrust my horns at his ribs, sending him face first into the rocky wall. 'This rut is over Hatari. Now let me go.'

Hatari, still dizzy and shaken, stumbled to his feet. *'Get him!'* he ordered his gang.

Waruhiu stayed at the opening of the rock to stop me from leaving, while Thairu, Shomari, Tuwile and Shinuni charged towards me. They split and circled me blocking my escape. As they closed in and pinned me tightly between them, Hatari started walking towards me, shaking his head to flick away a droplet of blood from his nostril. 'I will decide when this Rut is over,' he said, staring at me without blinking.

I tried to wriggle free of the gang, desperate to get away, but their grip was far too tight. If I couldn't get out of here, I'd at least want to go down fighting.

'Hold him!' Hatari yelled with anger in his eyes. The gang squeezed even tighter and Shinuni pressed the tips of his horns against my throat. 'When the herd hears how I defeated you, and that you ran off into the woodlands with pure embarrassment, I will be in charge. The vultures will have picked you clean before anyone in the herd even started to worry about you. And when I am leading this herd, your father and Talib will be cast out like the Nyumbus they are.'

'You won't get away with this Hatari,' I yelled. 'And this herd will never follow a loser like you.'

Hatari let out an angry grunt and took a step backwards. He dug his back hoofs into the dust, ready to charge at me.

There was a loud crack to our left. Waruhiu fell to the ground, blood pouring from a cut on the back of his head. He was out cold.

Talib entered the rocky tower, shaking his rear leg in pain. My father, Kwame and Jelani came in after him.

'Nice kick Talib,' said Jelani checking Waruhiu wouldn't be getting back up. 'Are you OK?'

'It stings a little, but it will pass,' he replied and smiled wryly to Jelani.

'Let him go!' shouted father.

'Keep hold of him,' Hatari told his gang, and he walked over to face my father. 'Typical. You have to get help from these filthy animals. You should learn to stick with your own kind Imamu,' he said looking over at both Talib and Kwame.

'You disgust me Hatari. I should never have trusted you. You will all be expelled from the herd for this, you mark my words. Now let Berko go.'

'You keep hold of him,' snapped Hatari, and the gang all squeezed tighter against me. 'I have been welcomed into the herd by the council,' Hatari continued, 'and I have beaten seven others to raise my ranking. You cannot banish me now.'

'Your ranking means nothing Hatari. You cannot move up the herd by cheating. And it is our word against yours, who do you think the council will believe?' he looked over to the gang. 'If you all want to follow Hatari you can, but you are no longer welcome with us.'

Hatari stepped closer to father. 'Fine! Then I will make you a deal. Just you and me Imamu. If I beat you I can remain within this herd, my boys too. If you beat me then we will leave and never return.'

'Fine...'

'Wait Imamu...' Jelani leapt in. 'You can't make a deal with Hatari. He disrespects our values. He ignores the rules. He can't be a part of this herd; he will endanger us all.'

Father looked back at Jelani and whispered something before turning back to look at Hatari, 'I accept your challenge Hatari. But you follow our rules. The rules our ancestors created. And your boys must let Berko go.'

'Fine,' he nodded sharply to the gang and they let go of me. I pushed away from them angrily and walked over to stand with the leaders.

Father and Hatari stood face to face staring right into one another's eyes. 'Make your move Imamu,' Hatari said.

Father took a step backwards.

'Wai...' I was about to call out to stop the fight but Talib stopped me.

'Your father knows what he is doing Berko,' he whispered, so I backed down.

CHASING THE RAIN

Father reared up on his hind legs. He brought his horns down on top of Hatari's head, buckling his knees beneath him.

It took a few seconds but Hatari finally got up. He shook his head and took a step backwards. He was about to rear when he dropped back down, looking defeated. He shook his head again to regain his focus and then looked up, before kicking a pile of dust into fathers face, filling his eyes and nose.

Father staggered backwards, shocked and disorientated. Hatari leapt forward, smashing his horns onto father's chest, sending him backwards into the dust. Hatari's Gang rushed over between us, kicking a cloud of dust into the air.

When the dust finally settled, father was led on the ground, his eyes streaming from the grit. Hatari was on top of him, forcing his hoof onto father's neck, crushing his throat. 'I didn't go any further when I did this to Talib, do you remember? But we were only children back then.' He pushed his hoof harder onto father's throat. 'But I will do a much more thorough job this time.' Father was now struggling to breathe.

'Get off him Hatari!' shouted Jelani, 'you will kill him.'

'Hopefully,' said Hatari with a sneer.

Shinuni turned to watch what was happening, so Jelani took the opportunity and butted the side of his head as hard as he could, sending him to the ground with a thud.

Thairu and Shomari broke their gaze on us all and in the confusion we were able to fight our way past the entire gang. Jelani, Talib and I fought them while Kwame went to help my father. He rushed past Shinuni, bashing his head with his shoulder, knocking him out cold, before charging Hatari. He rammed his long Spiral antlers at his side. There was a loud thud followed by a squelching rip and Hatari was thrown to the side and off father at great speed. He fell heavily to the ground with a dull thump, his body limp as it rolled over, and the dust all around him slowly turned dark crimson.

'Nyumbu,' shouted Tuwile as he charged at Kwame to take out his anger. Talib quickly swiped his rear hoof out as Tuwile ran past, catching him on the side of the head and sending him crashing onto the ground. His body was lifeless as it hit the dust and landed right next to Hatari.

The others ran over to them both and tried to wake them, but there was no response. They looked quickly towards the opening of the outcrop, where Waruhui was getting back to his hoofs, before trying to run, but Jelani and Talib cut them off.

Father finally got to his hoofs and stood over the two motionless bodies in the middle. 'This should never have happened,' he said to the gang with a struggle, his throat still painful. 'We follow the ways of our ancestors. The ways that have seen our troops survive for millennia. We are peaceful and loving. Violence only brings with it hate and suffering. We stick together; we are not like our enemies.' They tried to apologise but father cut them off quickly. 'You made a choice. You chose to follow Hatari and to hurt others. And in doing so you have offended the entire herd,' he looked down and shook his head solemnly before looking back up at them. 'In following Hatari in violence and disloyalty, his blood is on your hoofs.'

Three vultures circled over the rocky tower, occasionally peering in to look for a feast. Father made the four adolescents stand by the wall while Jelani went over and checked Hatari and Tuwile, pushing them gently with his hoof. He looked up at father and gave a slow, solemn shake of his head.

'You four... wait outside. And don't even think of running,' father said to the adolescents who walked out through the opening in the rock, whispering to each other about Hatari. 'Kwame, I owe you my complete gratitude,' continued father. 'And Talib?'

'I am so sorry Imamu, I was merely defending Kwame. I saw red when he used such words, I should have had more restraint.'

'You did a courageous act Talib, your quick thinking saved Kwame's life. Tuwile was too much like Hatari, who knows what he was capable of,' said father.

'Are you ok Berko?' asked Jelani.

'Yes. Thank you. I should never have accepted his challenge. I'm sorry father, you warned me, and you were right,' I said. 'How did you find me?'

'Nemsi tipped us off,' said Kwame. And we got here just in time. You conducted yourself well Berko. And Hatari showed his true colours.'

'We are deeply sorry for allowing it to get so far Berko,' added Talib. 'When I warned you he was looking to raise his ranking, I should have kept a closer eye on him. You know I would never let him harm you.'

'You saved my life, all of you, and for that I'm eternally grateful,' I said. 'But I should be saying sorry to you all. He could have become a leader, and worked with all of you. And it was all because of me.'

'Hatari and his assailants cheated Berko,' said father. 'The way he acted was shameful. It was not how the rut is intended. The displays are a way to demonstrate you have the skill and the strength to outsmart your opponent and render them powerless, as well as show your true character. You win with wisdom and prowess, not with violence. Hatari forfeited right from the start, including all of his previous displays. He could never gain respect by bullying his way to the top as he did. And getting his gang to help fight his battle just showed weakness, which is not a trait this herd looks for in a leader.'

'So what do we tell everyone about Hatari and Tuwile?'

'We tell them the truth,' said father. 'This should never have happened and I am saddened by what unfolded. But it was not your fault Berko, or ours. We are a peaceful species, as too are our closest friends. But when we are threatened by our enemies, our instincts help us to survive. I just never thought we would have to defend ourselves against one of our own.' He checked we were all ok before gesturing to us to exit the rocky tower. He stood aside and we all filed out through the opening. Just as he was about to follow, he turned back and looked to the skies. 'They are all yours.'

Out in the open, father faced the four adolescents. 'I hope you are all satisfied? Now start walking. And when you reach the herd, wait for us to meet you.' They turned and started walking with their heads lowered. 'And speak to no one.' They split apart while they walked; with such fear of my father, they didn't even talk to each other. When they were a little way in front father turned back to us. 'Come on; let's go back to the herd. We have a meeting to arrange.'

When we returned, Ayana came charging over to see me. 'Berko! You're ok. Thank the stars.'

'Ayana, can you go and fetch your mother?' Said Jelani before I could even answer her. 'And Amara and the children too. We are gathering the leaders. We are about to call a meeting.'

'Ok father. Can Berko come with me?'

'Not just yet, he needs to join us at the front.'

Ayana looked at me and I gave her a smile, but I had a knot in my stomach and wanted desperately to go with her. Father and the others started to walk away and called back for me to follow them. 'Bring those *enemies* with you Berko,' said Talib, disgusted to even look at them.

'Berko, please. We're sorry for what happened,' said Thairu. 'We were afraid Hatari would hurt us if we didn't follow his orders.'

'I'm sorry...' I started, but then I thought about what they'd done to me back there. 'You made your own beds; you have to lie in them. Now go.' I said, and shoved him forward.

All the leaders were gathered and father was telling them everything that happened. They all looked concerned and were touching their cheeks to each of those who were involved. When I arrived, they all came over and Idriis touched his cheek to mine. 'My dear boy, I am so glad to see you are ok. Terrible news about Hatari, just awful.'

I told father Thairu had just pleaded for forgiveness. That he said he acted through fear of Hatari.

'Do you believe him Berko?' He asked.

I thought for while but I decided I couldn't lie to my father. 'I don't. I feel he was just trying to get out of being punished for what he did. When he attacked me, he did so through choice. And it was him who tripped me for Hatari. He shows the same bad traits.' Father nodded and thanked me for my honesty before returning to the others to talk.

The herd started to gather for the announcement and Ayana came charging through the crowd with the rest of our families following. They all got right to the front to see that I was ok. Father and the other leaders approached the crowd and called for order.

Idriis started the meeting. 'As most of the males know, Hatari challenged Berko to a Rut today. He and his group have been using illegal tactics to try to win the respect of this herd. Imamu now has an important announcement for you all to hear. Please show your respects. Thank you.'

Father approached the front and addressed the herd. 'Thank you Idriis. It is not usual practice to report the Rut to the entire herd in this manner, but it is with great sadness that I have to report some grave news.' The crowd fell completely silent. 'The blood of Hatari and Tuwile is on the hoofs of their friends and accomplices Thairu, Shomari, Waruhiu and Shinuni.' The entire crowd gasped. 'Hatari chose to use force to try and win his displays illegally, and in doing so he disrespected our ancestors. As you have now heard, he challenged my son Berko to a display earlier today, but he was caught using methods that are not of our practices. And he relied on his group to help him defeat his opponents.' The crowd started to talk among themselves, shocked at the news.

'Quiet please,' said Idriis in a booming voice. 'Please Imamu, do continue.'

'Thank you. In the same way as all of Hatari's opponents in this Rut, Berko was gracious and respected the rules. However, Hatari and his gang used violence.' He went on to describe the events at the outcrop in detail, telling the herd exactly what had happened. 'When Hatari attempted to choke me, Kwame acted in my defence, stopping him with necessary force and in the process saving my life,' he turned to Kwame and bowed as a sign of true respect. The crowd then showed their respect to Kwame in the same way. 'Talib also had to use force to defend Kwame and the others from an attack by Tuwile.' Father bowed to Talib and again the crowd followed. 'This should never have happened. The Rut is about honour and respect. Hatari and his gang chose their path and in doing so rewrote their fate.'

The crowd started to talk among themselves before a female wildebeest at the front shouted 'I don't want those anywhere near my son during the rest of the Rut,' signalling towards the four adolescents. Then others started shouting out in support of her, stating they didn't want them to be around any of us.

'The leaders have made their decision,' shouted Idriis over the increasing volume. 'They are to be exiled from the herd; they will have to live the rest of their days on the edges of our society.'

'But that was Hatari's punishment and look what happened today,' shouted another member of the crowd.

Father went over and said something quietly to the Abasi, the oldest leader of the council. Abasi nodded and father approached the crowd again. 'Exile means they are no longer welcome into this society. However, given the true darkness of their intentions today, we are going to impose the four of them are banished from the herd entirely. This means that they can no longer trek with us, they cannot feed in the same grasslands or drink from the same lakes. They must survive on their own.'

'But that's not fair, we...' Thairu tried to interject.

'You are no longer our concern,' Idriis said, cutting him off, and the crowd huffed in agreement.

Father turned to look at the gang and continued 'in this herd we are loving, we are courteous and above all we are loyal. We look out for each other and we always follow our ancient practices. Practices that have seen us thrive for centuries. We wildebeest are a strong troop, but it is our friends and our allies that make the herd what it truly is.' Father turned back to face the crowd once again. 'Hatari led these four astray. But they knew right from wrong, and they chose to follow him down the path of violence. Thairu has shown himself to be like Hatari, both in his attitude and in the choices he made. The others are no different.' He lowered his head solemnly. 'I am truly saddened by the events we witnessed today. It is always difficult to lose one of the herd to one of our enemies, but this was far worse.' He raised his head again and addressed the crowd. 'We pride ourselves on our ability to live in peace, so what upsets me most of all is that we had to use anger to solve an issue within the herd...' he paused and then asked Jelani to take the four of them out of his sight. He took a deep breath and spoke to the vast crowd in a much lighter tone. 'I am really sorry to everyone; this has disrupted our rut for long enough. There are displays to be won and fun to be had. So please everyone return to the plains, continue our traditions and try to forget this day.' He bowed his head to indicate he'd finished the meeting and the crowd started to disperse, all talking about the events and speculating about the gang.

Father walked over to Thairu and the others and said 'you can now leave. Head south through the woodlands. You are no longer welcome to walk among us. You will feed on the scraps the herd leave behind, and you will drink only from pools formed by the rain. You have brought shame upon this herd and disgrace upon your families. It will take a long time, but the herd will heal from the dark events of this day. And you will carry that guilt for the rest of your lives.' He turned his back on them as a sign of utter disrespect. They all left slowly, and in complete silence.

By the time the rut had ended, I'd raised my ranking within the herd. I was challenged by three males in total. First, one from my year group who I defeated; this didn't add much to my ranking but we both just wanted to experience a true rut. My second opponent was a few years older; he was much larger and a lot stronger than me. I gave him a good run but I had to bow out and accept defeat. Then my third opponent was older still, and he was strong. We displayed for quite a long time. He got some good hits in and I was able to counter his blows well. I managed to use the technique my father had showed me and outsmarted him. It gave me a good advantage and when I landed a solid blow to the top of his head, he submitted and bowed out. He was a high ranking male so I was able to move up in my standings within the herd. The rut enables us to ascertain dominance and shows the others where we stand in relation to them. It also proves our masculinity, so it is after the rut is over and our ranking points are tallied, that the females start to look at us all a little differently. Especially us first timers.

Two young females came and spoke to me; they were around my age but must have been from a different drove because I didn't recognise them. They were having trouble holding a conversation as they kept giggling whenever they tried to talk to me. The taller of the two kept nudging the other to get her to ask me something, but then she would go shy and look down at her hoofs. Finally the tall one spoke, 'we saw your display with the large male, you were really impressive,' and she giggled again. I felt my face get warm and thanked them quietly; I then looked down at my hoofs too. Then the other one said 'we are going to be grazing among the flowers later, would you like to join us in the meadow?'

'I have to meet with the elders soon; they want to talk to me. I will probably be with them for most of the afternoon. So maybe catch up a little later? I'm really sorry.'

'Um... yeah sure. Ok, see you around Berko,' said the smaller of the two and they walked off towards the meadow, heading to a group of higher ranking males. I felt awful for turning them away but I knew they would soon forget all about me.

'Shame about your meeting,' said Ayana behind me. I turned around, startled.

'Hey, I've missed you these last few days.' I looked back to see that the two females were out of sight. 'How long were you stood there?'

'Oh not long, I came when you told them about your meeting. I've not seen them before,' she said with a huff. 'So what's your meeting about this time?' She seemed different, slightly quiet.

'I don't have a meeting Ayana. I just wanted to get rid of them. I don't want attention from anyone just because of the rut.'

'I didn't think you were even going to take part? and yet I hear you challenged three other males. Not to mention what happened with Hatari and his gang,' she said with an angry tone.

'I didn't challenge anyone Ayana. They challenged me... And it's true; I wasn't going to take part in the rut! *Especially* after my experience with Hatari. But it was only for a bit of fun, I just got caught up in the celebrations.' She looked upset so I tried to change the subject. 'I tried to find you after the leaders' announcement. You disappeared through the crowd. I haven't seen you this whole time.'

'Yeah well, I was with some friends.' She started to turn and walk away again.

'So... have you spoken to any of the males since the rut?'

'What? Why would you ask me that?' She snapped as she turned back to face me.

'I don't know? It's what the females do isn't it? It's tradition or whatever.'

'I'm not really interested in the traditions. I don't want to go and talk to some male because he's suddenly *so* masculine. It's ridiculous,' she looked down at her hoofs.

'Ayana...' I paused. 'I'm sorry. I should have told you I was facing Hatari.' She turned away a little. 'But you know males aren't supposed to tell the females about the Rut,' I moved closer to try and look at her. 'I was angry he'd been allowed back into the herd. And I knew how uncomfortable that had made you feel. He was breaking the rules, so I thought if I accepted his challenge, I could prove it to my father so Hatari could be caught and banished for good...' I paused again. 'Hatari said I was out of my depth. I guess he was right after all.' She looked up at me and had a tear in her eye. 'What is it Ayana?'

'I almost lost you Berko. I only heard about your Rut with Hatari from Imari. I didn't believe it, and I didn't think you'd accept a challenge from him of all wildebeest, when you know what he's like. But when I couldn't find you anywhere, and then I saw those four being lead back with the leaders, I feared the worst.' She looked to the side. 'When your father was saying all that stuff in the announcement, what Hatari had done, and what he'd been planning. It made me realise...' She paused and then she looked back down at the ground again. 'Look, you are not out of your depth Berko. You show strength and bravery, the signs of an amazing leader. But you are only on your third journey. And you don't need to prove yourself to anyone; the herd can all see what a great wildebeest you have become. I was so relieved to see you were ok, but I was also upset. If Hatari had succeeded, I'd never have seen you again. And you didn't even tell me about it.' She turned to look at me again; she stared right into my eyes. 'I can't lose you Berko.'

'I'm so sorry Ayana; I never meant to make you feel like that,' I looked into her eyes. 'When Hatari's gang had me pinned and I knew he was about to...' I could see tears bubble up in her eyes again. 'I thought of only one thing. The most important thing in my life.'

'What was that Berko?' she asked with a break in her voice as the tears rolled down her face.

'I thought of you Ayana.'

'Me?' she said with surprise.

'I've admired you for so long. But I've always been too scared to say anything. And this week I was finally feeling brave enough to mention it, but you were always rushing off. I figured you were interested in someone else, that's why I asked if you'd spoken to anyone since the Rut.'

She looked at her hoofs, still crying and was scratching at the dirt in front of her. 'I was jealous Berko. I've liked you for as long as I can remember, but when you sounded interested in Zuri I assumed I would be the last wildebeest you would look at. I've heard so many females talking about you this morning, and then I saw you talking with those two. I thought you were starting to build a harem,' she looked up at me. 'You're able to have your pick of the females. Every female in the herd wants to be with you, even females form other droves. Why aren't you interested?'

'Because I only want to share my life with you Ayana.'

She looked at me in complete shock and then she slowly approached and pressed her cheek to mine tenderly, 'so those two you were talking to? You weren't going to meet them later?'

'No, like I said, I don't want to talk to any females I don't know, just because of the rut. Besides, they're like all the others; they only want one thing. To choose a mate so they can have offspring with a dominant male, but they don't have feelings for whoever they choose.

The spirits choose us through love. The love we've been given as children and the love we show to others. The choice of father doesn't influence the outcome of the child. It is nurturing and care.'

She sniffed and blinked hard to try to stop the tears, 'I think you've been spending too much time with the leaders Berko. You're starting to sound like one of the elders,' she laughed and then sniffed again. She then gave me a playful nudge which broke the tension between us completely.

'I think you're right,' I mimicked Idriis' voice and Ayana giggled again. 'I've missed my time with you Ayana. And I've missed being myself.'

'Me too. And I'm sorry I didn't just come and talk to you like I always have in the past.'

'I'm sorry too. I just want us to go back to how we were.'

'Well in that case... *you're it*,' she said and nudged me aside before she ran off into the distance.

'Hey, I wasn't ready. Wait up,' I called and chased after her. She led me into the meadow and we dashed through the tall grasses. The sweet smell of the flowers was all around me and Ayana's laughter blew through on the wind. She vanished through the mixture of colours, but I soon caught her scent on the breeze. I came out into an opening where the grasses and flowers were flattened and the sunlight shone through the petals, hitting the ground in an array of different colours.

Ayana was stood on the opposite side and she smiled as I approached. I kissed her cheek but I didn't say a word, and for the first time in months I felt truly free.

5
The Mighty Mara

After the rut had ended, the herd remained on the sacred plains for two weeks. This gave the males and females enough time to officially pair up or build their harems. Everyone else enjoyed the meadows and grasslands and took pleasure in the serenity this area had to offer. The stay also gave me the opportunity to spend time with Ayana and rekindle our friendship after the last few weeks. With me going off to my lessons all the time and Ayana thinking I wasn't interested in hanging out, it had become frayed. But following our time in the meadow and with our true feelings for each other now in the open, it was much easier to talk.

I'd always loved how I could share anything with her, but as my feelings for her changed, I found it more difficult. I couldn't act the same in case I embarrassed myself, and I held back from telling her how I truly felt. But now we've gone back to our old ways. I can be myself, act silly, and if I say the wrong thing she still laughs, but I laugh with her. And when she does any of this stuff, I just love her that little bit more. I haven't been as happy as this for a long time, and now I have Ayana's love I am getting happier all the time.

The giraffe and rhinos made their way back to the Nusu Woodlands today. They are now going to start their own journey to the East, following these vast woodlands and taking advantage of their bountiful riches. It is always a sad time when the herd divides like this, but we know we will see them all again soon. Ndwiga, one of the giraffe, was thanking the leaders for guiding them to their sacred woods, and although they were laughing and joking a lot, you could feel the sadness in everyone. In a few days time the eland will also be leaving us so they can head to the vast lake to the west. The heat will become too much for them to bear as we travel north and the lake will provide them a safe haven before they travel east to rejoin our herd once more.

The herd have been preparing for tomorrow when we begin our trek north again. We are following the rains as far as they will take us before they change direction and lead us back to where this journey started. The grasslands are becoming too dry and the meadow is starting to wilt. The mood is still good throughout the herd and the rut is still being thought of as a success, and by tonight the new relationships should all be forged and our species should be ready to set forth in the newly formed groups.

Ayana and I decided to take my siblings out for the afternoon to give my parents some time on their own. Imari was really excited because I promised to take them away from the herd, to play in the open grasslands. Karamu kept asking Ayana why we hadn't spent much time with them recently. 'We have had to do grown up stuff, we're not as lucky as you and your brother.'

CHASING THE RAIN

'Like what? What have you had to do?' she asked enthusiastically.

'Karamu, go and catch Imari, before he gets too far ahead.' I said to save Ayana any more embarrassment and she looked at me and smiled to thank me.

We got to the grasslands and played Ampe for a while and it was nice to see my siblings enjoying the sunshine and having fun. We played a few more games and then chased each other around to burn off some of their energy before sitting in the dry grass to catch our breath. 'When we get nearer the rivers, we will have a chance to feast on fresh grass again.' I said to Imari who smiled at the idea of a meal he didn't have to chew all morning.

'Berko? Why do we have to keep walking all the time?' asked Karamu.

'To survive. We couldn't just stay here; there wouldn't be enough food for us all.'

'Why not?' she asked.

'Do you remember when I told you about the rain? How it brings life? Well, we are following the rains across this vast land. When the rain falls in the distance, we go to find what it's provided for us. If we're lucky, the rain will have soaked the earth and the plants will have grown up from the soil. While we feed, the rain moves on to provide for us all over again. So we follow it.'

'But all the troops go to the same place. If we split up, wouldn't the food last longer?' asked Imari.

'We wildebeest can sense the rain; we know when it has fallen. And the rain helps the herd. We are the herd Imari, all of us. And by working together we help the rains, and the earth.'

'How? he asked.

'Well, the zebra feed on the tall, drier grasses that you don't like.'

'Yuk, it's horrible. It's hard to chew,' said Karamu screwing up her face in disgust.

'Well the zebra love it, it's their favourite food, and that clears the way for us and the eland. When we feed, it exposes the fine, lush shoots of grass beneath, your favourite. Then the gazelle, with their delicate mouths pick out the fine shoots that we leave behind. Once we've all eaten our fill, the elephants will kick up the ground and make huge plumes of dust. They love to feed on the roots of the grasses and spread the seeds as they go. And then it is all ready for the rains to come and soak it. So it will grow for us again when we return. So you see that's why we all need one another. And why we make such a good herd. We wildebeest couldn't do this alone, and neither could our friends. So by living in harmony, we all help each other to survive. We've long believed that although we all look different, we are in fact all the same. Our spirits know that too, which is why they guide us with the rains and choose our fate.'

'So if we are all the same, why was Hatari so horrible to the others?' asked Imari.

'Unfortunately he didn't see our friends as part of the same herd. And he didn't consider them equal. He and his friends thought we would be better off if we only stayed with the wildebeest and splitting would benefit us, even if it didn't benefit our friends.'

'But that isn't fair.'

'And that's why they are no longer here. They chose to ignore the guidance of their spirits and tried to change their fate. It's good to forge own path in life, but not if that path leads you in the wrong direction. Their actions and behaviour were wrong, and they have to wait and see what fate has planned for them. They are on the other side of the woodlands now while the spirits decide.'

'But they won't be able to eat anything,' Karamu said compassionately.

'And only then will they realise what they lost,' I indicated for them both to come closer. They edged forward and looked up at me expectantly. 'I want you to promise me that you will always be kind to all of our friends. When you go and play with Talib's children, or Kwame's and Afia's, you'll treat them the same as you want to be treated yourself.'

'Of course,' they both said together.

I touched my cheek to theirs softly and lovingly. 'I am very proud of you both, and I am happy you are my siblings,' I said. 'Come on, we better start heading back before mother gets worried,' and they both stood up and set off towards the herd.

Ayana and I followed a little way behind watching as they walked closely together, Imari protecting his sister all the time. 'You are a good brother Berko,' she said and pressed herself against me lovingly. 'They really look up to you.'

At first light my family were woken by Ndwiga. He'd run across the grasslands from the woods and was panting heavily. 'Imamu, I need to speak with you.'

'What is the matter Ndwiga? What is so important?'

'I can't speak here Imamu; I must see you urgently, away from the youngsters.'

'Ok, give me a moment.' He turned to mother. 'Keep Karamu and Imari here; don't let them get up just yet. I need to see what the fuss is about.' He started to head over to meet Ndwiga so I got up and followed at a distance.

Father met with him and Jitu, one of the other giraffe and they started to speak quietly, so I moved closer to listen to their conversation.

'We were feeding at the edge of the woodlands, grazing on the foliage, when we saw a wildebeest alone in the grass,' said Jitu. 'We could see he was not sleeping but seemed to be in a lot of pain. I wanted to check on him but as Ndwiga said, there could be dangers lurking nearby. So we came to tell you at once Imamu.'

'Thank you. Both of you. I will gather some of the others and go and check it out. You did the right thing.' They both turned and walked back towards the woodlands and I tried to quickly walk away but father turned and spotted me. 'Morning son... You can help me round up the others. And please let your mother know I have gone but keep an eye out for our return. I don't want you coming on this trip Berko, I almost lost you once. I can't put your mother through that again.'

'Ok father, but please be careful.'

'I will. Thank you son.'

Father and some of the other leaders headed off for the woodlands before everyone had stirred. Ayana came over to ask what was happening, so I told her all I knew and we sat with my brother and sister to keep them entertained. Whilst father and I were gathering the other leaders, some of the herd must have overheard because there was chatter and speculation among them, and some were starting to get nervous. I tried my best to calm some of them down, telling them the leaders were just investigating something, but this seemed to just make matters worse. In the end Idriis called order and told the herd to calm down. They seemed to listen to him more than they did me. The herd was expecting to be heading north soon so the calm would be unlikely to last.

I sat back down with my siblings to keep them calm and Imari turned to me and whispered, 'this is like my dream Berko. But in my dream Thairu was here, bleeding.'

'Imari, shush, you will scare your sister. And we don't want the herd to panic.'

'Sorry.'

The leaders finally appeared from the woodlands and the chatter and speculation started again as everyone tried to see if they were all ok. The nearer they got we were able to see that Jelani had blood on his face. Ayana started to worry and tears were welling in her eyes so I tried to comfort her, but the leaders' slow pace made me fear the worst. Ayana got up and ran towards her father. Mbali called for her to stop, but she didn't listen.

'Berko, please go after her,' said Mbali.

I chased after Ayana but she was too quick. My heart was pounding but she reached the leaders before I could even catch her, and when she got there she burst into tears as she touched her cheek to Jelani's.

'Are you badly hurt Jelani?' I said through heaving breaths as I arrived.

'I am fine Berko. As I said to Ayana, it is not my blood.'

'What's going on?' I asked.

'Ndwiga was right; there was a wildebeest alone beyond the woodlands. It was Thairu,' said father.

'Thairu?' I paused, 'is he hurt?'

'He told us the four of them were honouring their friends with a late moonlit celebration in their memory. He said they often stayed up after dark with Hatari to discuss creating their new herd,' he looked over at Jelani who shook his head in disappointment. 'It saddens me. I knew Hatari was selfish, but I never thought he could be so reckless. He had never taken the time to teach those youngsters important skills or lessons. And they chose to celebrate at night on the open plains of the Simba Koppjes. They didn't stand a chance.'

'Why what happened?' I asked.

'Thairu said they were caught unaware. They were in the open when a pack of lions came silently upon them. They were ambushed from all angles.'

'So Thairu is ok though?' asked Ayana with real concern.

'Unfortunately not,' answered father. 'He managed to escape the grasp of one of the lionesses, and was able to hide in the long grass through the night. But his injuries were bad. He couldn't stand up; his leg was too badly injured...' he paused for a while. 'I almost felt sorry for him. Until he said that,' father said to the other leaders who all shook their heads in disapproval of Thairu's attitude.

'What are you talking about father?'

'We offered to bring him back. We were even going to allow him to travel with us again until he was well enough. But when we tried to move him he got angry at us. He shouted at Jelani and spat in his face, hence the blood. He said he would never return to our herd; he'd rather wait for the vultures.'

'He is foolish, and selfish. Just like Hatari,' said Jelani angrily.

'He told us to watch our backs; our enemies now know where the herd is.'

'How would they know? We are far beyond the Koppjes,' I said.

'As he ran to hide in the long grass, he shouted that they would never catch him beyond the woodlands. It is unclear if they would have believed him, but I am glad we are heading out today.'

'So what will happen to Thairu?' Ayana asked my father.

'With the injuries he has sustained, it is unlikely he will make it to the end of the day. And he refused to accept our help.'

'I do not understand how he was able to escape,' said Talib. 'If the pack of lions was as large as he said, and three were chasing him, then they would have easily brought him down. And they would not give up when he is already injured.'

'As I said, he is selfish,' said Jelani. I would not be surprised if he sacrificed his friends in order to make his escape.'

'I fear you could be right,' said father. 'We should go. We do not want to wait around if Thairu was telling the truth.'

The leaders headed back to report what had happened and announce that the herd needs to start the trek north, so I held back to walk with Ayana.

'That's horrible. I hope they didn't suffer,' I said

'After what they all did to you Berko, I feel like that was fate.'

'It's funny. This morning, Imari said the strangest thing.'

Back at the herd, there was still a lot of commotion. Everyone was searching desperately for loved ones, panicking when they couldn't find them straight away. The leaders were all trying to keep them calm while still urging them to prepare to leave. If the herd didn't begin to focus then the slightest thing could cause a mass panic, and the last thing we needed was a stampede.

We stayed close to mother and Mbali, and Ayana and I kept my siblings entertained to try to take their minds off what was happening all around us. I kept looking back towards the woodlands when I could see movement on the plains, but it was just the heat of the savannah causing my eyes to play tricks. The leaders of every drove finally managed to calm the herd. Each took charge of their group and peace was brought over the mass as one. My father and the others announced it was time to head north and the herd followed on warily.

The trek was eerily quiet. There's usually a low hum of conversation, but today was different. I could hear every hoofstep on the dry, hard ground. The swish of a tail deflecting an insect before it could bite the warm dusty skin of one of the animals nearby. The occasional screech of a buzzard echoed through the skies and the herd would look up before closing their eyes tightly at the brightness of the sun. It was now the end of the rainy season and the heat had returned with such ferocity that each bead of sweat was dried as soon as it appeared. As our hoofs touched the ground, the thin, dry surface cracked to reveal dark imprints from the soil beneath. Dust rose up between every animal and filled our nostrils and eyes, but we blinked through the grit and puffed out air to help us breath. We wildebeest are able to cope easily with this amount of warmth, but Kwame's family were clearly struggling. They'd spent much of the night feeding and the stress of this morning was taking its toll. We went to walk with them, to try to keep up their morale and help them to keep going.

My brother and sister spoke with Kwame's younger daughter and niece, but they were too tired to play. We spoke with his wife and her sister to make sure they were ok. 'We are finding it difficult this morning to stay with the herd,' said Binah, Kwame's wife.

'We are going to head west toward the great lake today. It's a couple of days early, but we need to start heading there now in case the temperature gets any higher. We can take refuge there for a while before heading east across the plains again,' said Eshi.

'Kwame is going to tell the others, we are going to change course after the next rest stop,' Binah added.

Ayana and I dropped back and spoke to Kwame's older daughter Hadiya so our mothers could talk with their friends. Karamu came and spoke to us, looking upset. 'Kinuka and Sabiha aren't coming with us. They said you're leaving Hadiya. Is it true?'

'Yes, we are heading to the vast lake. We would have been leaving in a couple of days Karamu, so it is only a bit early. But you will see them again. We will meet with you in the east.'

'But I'll miss you. And I like playing with them in the afternoons, when we stop walking.'

'You will still have your other friends to play with,' I said. 'And just think of all the stories you can tell each other when you meet up again.' I touched my cheek to hers. 'I know it seems like a long time until you will see them again, but that time will go by quickly. I promise.'

She pressed her body into mine lovingly and then went back to see her friends. Ayana came up to me and touched her cheek to mine and we continued our journey among the silent herd.

When we stopped to rest, our friends all came to say goodbye. I went and thanked Kwame for everything he'd done for me these past months.

'I look forward to seeing your progress when we meet again Berko. I am very proud of you.' He pressed his cheek to mine and then bowed to me jokingly. 'You are going to make a fine leader one day, when you finally have your growth spurt,' he winked.

'Thank you Kwame,' I said quietly and laughed.

The leaders all showed their respects to Kwame and his family by bowing together as they walked away. We all stood and watched as all of the eland amassed and walked towards the horizon and the entire herd bowed to them as one as they looked back to show we'll miss them all. Karamu put her head against me, upset they were all leaving and Imari tried to act strong, but when I asked if he was ok he turned away without speaking. The herd were sombre and struggled to get moving, and when we finally headed north again, the deathly silence hung heavily over us like the thick dark clouds of the Masika storms.

The leaders wanted us to push on until the afternoon to make good headway on the trek and get clear of the enemies from the previous night. News like this would often dampen our spirits, but I was actually looking forward to the trek. The further we could get, the further we could push the sad day behind us. And start looking forward to the future.

The herd slowed as the leaders scanned the area for a suitable resting place. The grass was good and there was plenty of water from several small streams running through the plain, so they advised us to stop and make camp for the night. The long continuous walk had made the sad events of the day easier to recall, and the herd had started to talk more freely once we'd stopped. The area had a calm atmosphere and its vast open plains made our chances much better.

There was talk of a ceremony that evening, to wish our friends the eland, giraffe and rhino safety for their journeys. The ritual would carry our spirits up to find theirs and pass on our love to guide them forward unharmed. It is an ancient practice we have done since the beginning of our herds' existence, where our love and our strength will guide those we respect, and theirs will be felt by us in return.

I took Imari to one side and asked that he look out for Karamu. 'She is still very upset about Kinuka and Sabiha. You always know how to make her laugh Imari. Try to keep her mind off it until the ceremony tonight.'

'Okay Berko, I'll play her at Ampe. I guess I could let her win this time,' he smiled and was about to go and find his sister.

'Imari, wait... Your dream. You said you dreamt of Thairu. What happened in your dream?'

'I don't know? I think he was bitten by a monster,' he said dismissively, and then he ran off to find Karamu.

The herd all grazed on the luscious grass and filled their bellies with cold water from the streams. The exhaustion from the long trek was felt in our legs, but it was blocked by elation to have reached such a beautiful part of the savannah. As the plain was bathed in a vibrant golden glow, the leaders came around to gather us all together. Everyone found their loved ones and gathered around the leaders in the warmth of the evening light. A vast clear circle was formed in the centre where the leaders all stood united. The ceremony was about to begin.

Idriis looked to the sun and watched it turn from yellow to orange as it lowered to the west of the plain. He turned to the other leaders and nodded slowly. They formed a vast ring by taking hold of the tail of the animal in front of them, and they walked slowly around Idriis without letting go. The rest of the herd sat on the ground and watched intently as Idriis began the ceremony with a sharp stamp of his hoof and a loud booming chant towards the skies, *'Roho!'*

Together, the leaders let out the same low, bellow from deep within their throats, *'Roho!'* It travelled out across the plain in all directions and the birds and insects on the savannah fell completely silent. The leaders began to trot and the dust beneath their hoofs was loosened and stirred up with every step.

'Roho!' the leaders chanted in rhythmic melody, and as their speed increased the dust became dense and danced up on the breeze as if it was alive. It got thicker with each hoofstep and everything turned ochre as the sun neared the horizon.

'*Roho!*' chanted the leaders as the pillar of dust began glowing bright orange, the dusk light dancing through it like fireflies.

'*Roho!*' they chanted. And the pillar danced as different shapes appeared from within it.

'The spirits! They are among us,' called Idriis as he looked towards the skies.

'*Roho!*' the leaders called once more in response, before they slowed their pace from a gallop to a trot and the dust hung low on the still warm air. And as the light of the setting sun changed from orange to red, different shapes appeared in the dust and moved all around it. The herd stared in wonder at the formations overhead, and the children named the different animals they could see through the rays of evening light.

The thick dust was finally dispersing, floating up to the skies on the light, warm breeze, and Idriis called out softly 'take our love and our strength and deliver them to our dear friends. Make them aware they are always in our thoughts and forever in our hearts.'

'*Rohooooo!*' the leaders' final chant echoed on through the air. They came to a halt and all turned in to bow to Idriis. They sat down in the clearing under the fading dusk light to watch the last of the dust disappear on a light breeze over the plain. The weight of our burdened hearts was lifted, and our wishes of hope were carried forth to all of our friends as they made their way towards their next destinations.

With the dawning of the new day, the darkness had lifted from the herd. There was a hum of talk among the herd about the ceremony, especially from the youngsters who had never had the chance to witness the spectacle before. The mood had changed and the herd was as bright as the sunshine that revealed the beauty in the area the leaders had chosen for our camp. The grass was green and the dew on the blades glistened in the morning sun. The streams were singing in the background as they trickled and splashed on the rocks, and there was plenty to eat and drink for everyone.

The leaders decided the herd should stay for one more day and allow those who were struggling, to rest and to eat. The day looked good. The children played and frolicked in the grasslands, playing Ampe and Mbube, and splashing around in the streams. The parents relaxed under the sun's warm rays and talked to old friends they had missed the past weeks. The leaders met on the plains to talk, but it wasn't all serious like it usually was, they spoke of past adventures and laughed as they reminisced about the eland, not once stopping to plan the journey or discuss their duties. The trek to the north finally felt more enticing and far less like a chore. We were as happy here as at the birthing grounds. And I hoped the feeling would last.

I spent more time with Ayana and we discussed our dreams for the future, and how we both look forward to the sacred lands in the north. We went for a walk to the furthest stream so we could be alone for a while, away from all our families and the screaming of children playing games. 'At least nothing can hide in this stream,' I said, and Ayana giggled as she touched the water with her hoof. We both drank from the stream and the water was sweet and cold. We sat on the grassy bank and stared up at the clouds. 'Do you think they got our message last night Berko?' she asked.

'The spirits would make sure of it.'

'The ceremony was amazing. But the look on your siblings' faces was better.'

'I know they haven't stopped talking about it all morning.'

'I am so glad we are back to normal Berko. I really missed spending time with you like this.'

'Me too. I don't ever want to be apart from you again Ayana. I love you, you know that don't you?' She didn't say anything; she just moved closer to me and pressed her body against mine. We spent the rest of the afternoon napping together in the hot glow of the sunshine, listening to the calming melody of the savannah.

I was startled from my nap by the cry of a bird overhead and as I jumped I woke Ayana too. 'Wow look how low the sun is, our families will be wondering where we are.'

'I'm sure they won't miss us, let's stay a little longer,' she said and we led back down as cosy as before. We talked about the north and the bountiful grasslands that will be waiting for us on our arrival. But we were both careful not to talk about the river in our path.

Cutting us off from the miles of green pastures of the sacred northern territory is the mighty Mara; a monstrous torrent which tests even the strongest of animals among us. My memory of the last crossing is patchy at best, a mixture of fear and adrenaline made sure of that. The adrenaline rushes through your body with as much intensity as the water of the Mara itself, and it helps you make the dangerous crossing alive, but it also turns the whole thing into a bit of a blur. That's not always a bad thing though; many have been lost to that mighty river and the dangers it hides beneath its surface. And although it's taken so many of our friends and family over the centuries, it definitely hasn't finished with us yet.

When Ayana returned to her parents, I took my siblings to the plains to play. They were acting out the ceremony and pretending they could spot different creatures in the air, pointing at the clouds and demanding they take their love to the eland. I challenged them to a game of Ampe to take their minds off it for a while, and when they got tired I led them to the nearest stream to have a drink before bed. I stood on the bank as the two of them were drinking. 'I want you to stick with me in a few days,' I said.

Karamu looked up with water dripping down her chin, 'why Berko?' she said, panting heavily, still tired from all the games.

'We're going to the best grasslands you have ever seen, and the streams will be colder and sweeter than you've ever had before. I want to be with you when we get there.'

'Better than these?' said Imari excitedly, before burping loudly.

'Yes, much better,' I laughed. 'But I think you better hold back a bit Imari,' he smiled at me and then burped again before going back for another drink. 'OK, I think you've both drank enough now. You'll be up all night.'

They both stopped drinking and shook the water from their faces. We walked back towards the herd slowly while I told them more about the amazing grasslands to the north, but I didn't want to scare them by telling them about the river. Just as we found mother Imari turned to me and whispered 'Berko, I think I need the toilet.'

Karamu giggled at him, 'Berko told you, silly...' then her eyes widened, 'Oh, I think I need to go now as well.'

Panic and confusion among the herd woke me at sunrise with a terrifying jolt. I sat up quickly and tried to look over the herd, my eyes struggling to adjust from their hazy stupor. Two adult wildebeest were calling for their children across the herd with fear in their voices as animals were dashing between them. Jelani rushed over to father and told him an urgent meeting had been called for the leaders to attend, and they had to go quickly. They headed towards the two frantic adults and swept them away to comfort them and help find their young. We waited for news of what was happening and none of us could eat until we knew. Then Idriis' voice boomed through the air as a meeting was called for all to attend.

'I am sorry for the short notice of this meeting, but it has come to light that this area is not as idyllic as we had once thought. These grasslands are swarming with Siafu and some of the youngsters have been suffering with terrible bites. We have decided to head out earlier than planned, so please prepare for our journey. Make sure you all eat as much as you can, but stay clear of the long grasses around the outskirts if you want to avoid the painful bite of these insects.'

Father joined us as we headed to get some breakfast and led me away from mother and my siblings, he looked around to make sure nobody was in earshot. 'The herd was ambushed last night Berko. A group of lions seized a few of the herd. Two young children, the same age as your siblings were snatched as they slept. And one of the older zebra too while he stepped away from the herd to drink. Their families have been told, but we asked them to keep it from the others for now, until we get to safer ground. We are not yet sure if it was the same group of lions Thairu mentioned.' He looked over to Imari and Karamu and then touched his cheek to mine for no reason. 'I need to talk to your mother, but please don't let your siblings near the grasses this morning. I don't want them seeing anything they shouldn't. They are far too young.'

'Ok father,' I said quietly.

The herd had calmed after the meeting and were saying how sad it was that such a beautiful area could be ruined by such small insects. Everyone prepared for the early start, rushing breakfast and drinking only a mouthful to keep them going. A sound of rustling filled the air as all of the herd were shaking to make sure no bugs were hiding within their coats. The older animals had realised something was wrong; a few driving ants would never have caused this much worry among the leaders, but after the commotion when Duni was taken, they know better to discuss what could have really happened. If this got out, the herd would likely panic.

The early start gave us all a massive boost of energy to journey north. The leaders' tactics worked well and

CHASING THE RAIN

everyone was excited to get to better grazing land so were happy to march without stopping. There was positive talk among the group too, and many were still reminiscing about the ceremony, saying the eland must have done a great ceremony for us, as our spirits were high this morning. We barely stopped all day, grazing on the move and drinking whenever we passed a stream. The leaders were taking turns to monitor the outskirts of the herd, making sure there were no lions trailing us, and when I walked with father during his survey, he said 'the lions should have had their fill, so by the time they are hungry again, we should be clear of them.

There were no further attacks on the herd over the next two weeks and our spirits remained high. Our trek had brought us to within touching distance of our biggest challenge. So we were going to take refuge at a well known spot further north, and rest for a few days before making the final approach to the Mara River. We were all getting nervous the nearer we got, as we knew the dangers the river can throw at us. But we also knew our biggest reward was on the other side.

I kept telling my siblings about the incredible grasslands to the north and that when we get there we would stay for many weeks with a seemingly endless supply of lush grass and flowers to keep us fed. When I told them it would be ages before we had to walk again once we were in the sacred territory, they beamed with excitement. But I still couldn't bring myself to tell them what lied in our path. I couldn't risk putting fear into them in case it scared them too much to make the crossing.

When we arrived at our rest stop, the roar of the Mara was hanging in the air. But everyone was too happy with the area to let it worry them. The grasses had been saturated by recent rains and the shoots were succulent and sweet. They would provide lots of energy for the crossing and keep our minds solely focused on our bellies.

I joined my family for the evening and sat while father told my siblings about the coming days. 'I want you both to stay with your brother. We will be making another crossing of a river. It is like the last large crossing you did, do you both remember that?' They both nodded. 'But this one is wider and much faster, which means the current will be very strong. Your mother will be with you, as will Mbali and Ayana; they have already told me they are going to keep an eye on you. But I do not want you being silly. I want you to concentrate and get across safely. Do you both understand?'

'Yes father,' they said together.

'Now get some rest for the morning. You both need to be bright and alert.' They both curled up together in the grass. He touched his cheek to mothers and then gestured for me to come with him to the open plains.

'Berko, you did a fantastic job helping us at the last crossing, all of the leaders were very impressed. But this time I want you to use the skills I taught you to keep our family safe within the water. There is going to be too much going on, and far too many bodies in the river for me to keep an eye on them all. I trust you completely, and I know you will take good care of our family as well as Mbali and Ayana as they make their way across the Mara.'

'I won't let you down father.'

'You will need to be far more careful this time Berko. This river is extremely dangerous. And our enemies will be expecting us. They know we cannot fight our instincts. And they know there are great rewards for our kind on the other side. So it is impossible for them to resist coming too. I will be on the banks watching for them, but you need to be vigilant for me in the water. Make sure you scan for all of the enemies I warned you about, both in the water and on the far bank. You are a brave young wildebeest Berko. I know you will make me proud in there.'

'Thank you father,' I said quietly. 'I will do my best for you.' We touched cheeks and then headed back over to mother, but none of us spoke about the river for the rest of the evening.

Over the next two days, we headed to the water twice, only to return to the grasslands again. The leaders had found us a safe place to cross but the herd were struggling with the idea of entering the water. The other droves had now made it to the grasslands and the number of bodies in the area was high, but seeing everyone together again was easing the tension of the situation.

Being the lead drove, we kept going right to the edge of the bank and waiting, but those at the front still weren't making the final move. Father said they were nervous of the jump and were still assessing it for themselves. The banks were high and the river was so much wider than any other we have to cross. According to the seekers, there are flatter places to enter the water, but it would take the herd around a day and a half to get there. This would put us so far off track that it would hamper our trek to the northern area. Father assured me the herd knows what they are doing and would make the crossing in good time. But it made me anxious whenever we turned back.

It was the third day in the grasslands. Our share of the grass was getting low so we couldn't stay there much longer. The leaders had headed back to the river to check the crossing point was still safe. My siblings were getting more scared about the river now they had actually seen it and I was doing my best to keep them calm. Ayana could see I was struggling and helped me by talking to them about the grasslands on the other side, and the games we would play when we got there.

Jelani came into view from the direction of the river and gestured for us all to follow. 'Hopefully we will cross today. Stay close, both of you,' I said excitedly to my siblings to hide my nerves as best I could.

As the animals at the front of the herd reached the high bank, they stopped, frozen to the spot as they had so many times. The rest of the herd knew there wasn't enough food left on this side to sustain us all now the herd was at full mass, so this was our last chance to find the courage to cross this menacing torrent.

We couldn't ignore our instincts any longer and the thought of fresh food on the other side was driving us on. The herd edged forward, jostling for position among all the bodies. There was nowhere for any of us in the middle to go and some of the herd started to panic.

The droves joining behind us were pushing the group further forward as they followed their instincts to cross too. And as the numbers on the bank became critical, we had no other choice but to go. The first row was nudged over the bank and some of them slipped down to the water's edge on the dry crumbling dirt.

The next row of animals leapt right into the river from the bank so they wouldn't injure anyone below, or push them into the raging current. There was a roaring splash as they entered the torrent, and the release on the precipice caused us all to jolt forward, pushed and shoved from all the bodies behind us. I called for my siblings to stay close and stretched my head high to see how much further we had to go to the sudden drop.

On the bank I helped the females make the jump safely by holding back the raging stampede for the shortest time with my body turned sideways towards the flow of animals. Mother and Mbali leapt in first, and they helped to steady Ayana as she entered the water at great speed.

'Ready... jump!' I shouted, and my siblings and I leapt into the water together. The river was deep and our heads went right under the surface, the cold shocking our bodies to the core. As we bobbed to the top and the muddy water washed over my face, I swished my tail for them both to grab in their teeth. It was too deep to touch the bottom and I had to use all my strength to swim across with them both clinging on for dear life.

Part of the way across there was a huge rush of water to our right. An adult wildebeest was launched out of the water by a large crocodile hiding beneath the surface, and as he struggled free of its huge jaws, he fell right on top of us. Terrified, my siblings thrashed in the water to get away, but Imari was knocked beneath the surface by the large animals' rump. He lost his grip on my tail and was swept right under by the strong current.

'Imari!' called Talib from the far bank; he had made the crossing safely and was assisting from the other side. I looked around for my brother but I couldn't see him anywhere. Karamu panicked and was splashing with her hoofs, trying desperately to get back to where we came from. Father shouted for me to continue to the other side, so I turned my head and grabbed Karamu by the tail, dragging her towards the other bank.

'Imamu, I can see him. I am going after him,' called Talib, and he leapt from the bank and charged along the shallow edge of the muddy river.

I managed to get Karamu safely to the other side and Ayana helped to drag her up through the crumbling dirt. Mother tried her best to calm Karamu but she was shaken by the whole thing, and was terrified for Imari.

'I have to go and check on them,' I said, tearing off down the bank, ignoring my family's pleas for me to stop.

I caught up just as Talib was dragging Imari through the water by his tail. I was relieved as I saw my brother scrambling to the edge. And although he was shaken, he was fine. Talib got him to the bank and pushed him out of the water with his head, so I dragged Imari up the bank and onto dry land; he was shaking and crying with fear.

Talib headed back along the water's edge to a lower part of the bank. He stepped into the soil to get a good hoofing when part of the bank broke loose beneath him and he slipped backwards, with clumps of mud rolling down and splashing in the water all round him. As Talib's rump broke the surface, there was a roar as the water beside him exploded in a burst of foam. A large crocodile lunged through the current, sending an earth brown spray high into the air. The crocodile rolled over, clamping its jaws closed on Talib's hock.

'Talib, hold on,' I cried, trying desperately to get down the crumbling bank to grab his hoof with my mouth.

'Go back Berko. Don't be foolish,' he shouted as he was dragged over onto his side by the ferocious creature. He let out a deep, agonising roar as he tried to tear his leg free of the animal's jaws. He kicked the crocodile hard on the muzzle with his free leg and it loosened slightly with the shock. Talib tugged his leg free, tearing the flesh, and started to drive his front hoofs into the mud, his muscles tightening as he hauled himself up. He pulled himself free of the silt and reeds and the water was swirling and bubbling all around him. There was a deafening thrash as the crocodile leapt up and grabbed his hoof once more. The water beside him surged up as a second crocodile lunged out through the muddy froth and grabbed Talib by the snout. I quickly hid Imari's eyes with my entire body and ushered him up the bank, telling him to lie completely still in the tall grass. I rushed back to the water to try to help Talib get out, but when I got there he had vanished. Talib and both the crocodiles had disappeared beneath a swirling crimson current and I fell into the sodden dirt with a throbbing ache within my heart.

Imari broke down and sobbed hysterically into the grass. I tried to stay as strong as I could and told him that everything was fine, but it was a struggle to keep myself from crying too. 'It's all my fault,' he said through the tears.

'Stop that Imari. You stop that right now,' I said loudly. 'You can't blame yourself for what happened. You did nothing wrong, do you hear me?'

'Ye... ye... yes Berko,' he said, but then he broke down again.

We both headed back slowly to the others and mother came charging over to meet us. 'Oh thank the stars,' she cried. 'I feared the worst.' She tried to stop Imari from crying but couldn't manage. When she looked up and noticed we were alone her eyes widened. 'Talib? Where is he?' I swallowed hard and held back the tears, but I said nothing, just pressed my cheek to hers and sobbed uncontrollably.

Once I'd calmed down, I ran to assist Jelani and the other leaders on the north bank by keeping watch and helping the other animals onto dry land. Father spotted me over the spray and nodded to me. He shouted something but I couldn't hear him over the splashing of hoofs in the merciless river.

The herd charged though the water towards us as they were shoved to the side. Screams rang out as those in the middle fell backwards and beneath the torrent. Through the spray a large hippo charged, splitting the herd and throwing bodies in all directions. We helped some of them up the bank and got them to safety while the others quickly turned back and headed for the opposite side. An adult wildebeest, stuck in the middle of the river was pulled to her side and under the water as the ridged back of a crocodile broke the surface.

At the water's edge, a small hippo was screaming to the adult in fear. She charged again to get to her baby, knocking the crocodile beneath the current with a heavy foot.

The female wildebeest burst through the water's surface, splashing her hoofs around as she tried to stay afloat and catch her breath.

The large hippo swept around angrily and stood between her baby and the crocodile and with a deep growl she rushed at it, grabbing its entire head within her jaws and pushing it under the water.

The female wildebeest got closer to us, so Jelani and I rushed down the bank to help her to safety.

The hippo let go of the crocodile but had injured its head badly, leaving it helpless on the muddy bank of the Mara. Her baby walked out of the river as she ran over, scooping it away from the water's edge. They walked down the bank and away from us all, and our leaders further down thanked her as she passed.

The herd restarted their crossing as if nothing had even happened, leaping into the water from the top of the bank once again.

Father and the other leaders entered the water with the last of our drove and we met them on our bank as they exited the water. 'Is Imari ok Berko? You didn't answer me before,' said father.

'Yes he's shaken, but he's safe...' I paused and lowered my head to hide my sadness.

'And Talib? Is he ok? I couldn't see him through the spray. I need to thank him for what he did for Imari.'

'He... He saved Imari father.' I said with a break in my voice. 'He...' I tried to continue. But I couldn't find the words to tell him what happened. Instead I just broke down and father pressed his cheek to mine. It was the first time I had ever seen my father cry.

The herd got to the plains on the other side and were able to rest in the sun. We spotted mother and my siblings so father headed over to assure them we were ok. Ayana stood up and ran over to greet me lovingly. 'Why did you go back Berko? You scared me to death.'

'I did it for Talib.' I said to her. 'I know it sounds silly, but after what he did for Imari, I wanted to honour him in some way.' She touched her cheek to mine.

Mbali was upset as Jelani confirmed what had happened and asked if she had seen Talib's family. They were over on the far side of the grasslands so he and father said they had to go and speak to her. 'Berko, do you feel you could speak with his wife. I am sure it would mean a lot to her if you could,' father said.

'Yes I will try,' I said nervously.

When we got over to them, her daughter was playing joyfully with her cousin, awaiting Talib's return. 'Shirika, may we speak with you?' said father. She looked up at him and her expression quickly changed. She knew the news wasn't good.

'Oh please tell me he is ok Imamu,' she said, beginning to cry.

'I am so sorry Shirika,' father said softly, and she broke down. Jelani went over to Talib's daughter Zarifa, to bring her over to her mother.

'How did this happen?' she asked my father and he turned to me. I nodded to him and sat beside her.

'Imari was swept away Shirika,' I said, holding back tears of my own.

'Oh please no. Not Imari. Please tell me he is ok Berko,' she looked straight into my eyes.

'Yes he is fine. But only thanks to Talib. He rushed to my brother's aid Shirika. He didn't think twice to go in after him. By the time I'd caught up, he'd managed to catch Imari and get him to safety,' my voice cracked as I held in the tears. 'He got him out of that river unharmed. I will never forget that Shirika.'

She pressed her cheek to mine tightly.

'I am forever grateful Shirika. For it not for Talib's bravery Imari would not be here now. Imari feels awful, we all do. I know nothing can make this right, but we will always be here for you,' added father, and he bowed to her in respect.

'Thank you Imamu. Please, don't put this upon yourself; you have helped us so much in the past,' she touched his cheek. 'I will come and speak to Imari soon. Talib would have only done what was right. And I know he was brave, he was the strongest zebra I knew. With a heart as large as the savannah.'

We all touched Shirika lovingly on the cheek before we left her alone with Zarifa and the rest of her family; she said she wanted to break the news to them herself before the meeting at sunset. We headed back to our families in complete silence, seeing Talib's family like that was difficult even for father.

As the sun was dropping, the herd began to gather. The meeting was soon to begin and there was a sense of sadness hanging in the air. It is customary for these meetings to be held after the Mara crossings. The leaders have much to report and it is only right that our respects are paid at this time. Once the herd had all settled around the leaders, Idriis thanked us all and introduced my father to come and speak to the crowd.

'Thank you Idriis. And thank you all for coming,' said father in a low solemn tone. 'It is my duty to report today's events to you all. I would first like to congratulate everyone for making the crossing safely and quickly despite the treacherous conditions today. The river was flowing faster than usual and you all did an incredible job of working like a true herd, helping those around you when they were in trouble...' he paused and lowered his head, the crowd fell deadly silent. Finally he looked back up and continued. 'It is with great sadness I have to report the loss of many of our friends and family members. We tried to avoid our enemies as best we could, but as you all know, they will always find us. Within the river, there were many casualties; most of them from the crocodiles and sadly some were overcome by the raging current. And we also lost more of our loved ones on the banks of the river, taken by the lions and hyenas. It is always a difficult time for us all and we need to stick together to help those among us who have felt some kind of loss today.'

Father looked towards Shirika and Zarifa in the front row of the crowd and nodded to her lovingly. She nodded back and he looked once again over the herd to continue. 'You will have noticed that Talib is not standing here with us. I would like to take this moment to wish his wife and daughter my deepest condolences. He...' Father had to pause and look away to suppress his sadness. 'Talib was one of my dearest friends,' he continued, his voice broken. 'In fact I think I would struggle to find anyone among us who couldn't say the same. As Shirika said to me today, he had a heart as large as the savannah, and I think you have all been lucky enough to experience the love he had to offer. He was always there for all of us and has touched all of our hearts. We lost him today, but we will never forget him.' Father bowed in respect. 'He always showed bravery and loyalty in abundance. He saved my son Imari from the mighty Mara River and for that I am eternally grateful.' The entire herd got to their feet and bowed as one. 'I will now hand over to Idriis to begin the ceremony for all of the fallen.'

'Thank you Imamu,' he bowed to father and then he turned to face the crowd. 'We will send our love and our wishes. Their spirits will be called and released to the stars for all eternity.' All of the leaders bowed together and the herd followed. The leaders then stood and bowed again; doing the same for each of our loved ones we lost. The herd followed their lead and the wind was stirred with the undulations of every bow. Upon the breeze, the dust was carried, lit by the suns last rays of light. And as it billowed and swirled above our heads, our wishes were said and our love sent up with them. The herd took one final bow and the dust hung above us, dancing peacefully on the breeze. We all sat on the ground as one large loving family and watched in silence as our loved ones' spirits rose up to the skies, to make their final journey and sit among the stars.

6
The Sacred Territory Calls

The herd had been on the move for six full days with barely a rest, the draw of the northern territory too much for us all to resist. Ayana and I had been spending a lot of time with my siblings, keeping their morale up so they could manage the pace of the excited herd. Imari was less withdrawn after Shirika spoke with him and explained he was in no way responsible for what happened. 'Talib saved you Imari because he loved you,' she'd told him. 'He was always impressed by the way you supported our daughter Zarifa, like she was your own sister. He wouldn't want you to be sad for his loss; he would want you to be strong for your family and for your friends. And above all he would want you to follow your true spirit.' She pressed her cheek to his and whispered something into his ear. His eyes widened at whatever she'd whispered and he smiled broadly. It was the first time I'd seen him smile since before the crossing.

When the herd finally stopped for the night, I asked Ayana to watch my sister so I could talk to Imari alone and make sure he was ok. Although he had been happier, there were still times he'd stared into the distance, and I was worried about him. I led him to a patch of long grass away from the herd. 'I've missed your smile Imari. It was good to see you happy again. If you ever need to talk, away from mother and father, you know you can just ask.'

'Is it true Berko? Could Talib see our fate?' He said, as if he didn't even hear what I'd said.

'I know he was able to see the spirits and father respected him for his foresight. But why do you ask that Imari?'

'It's just something Shirika said. She said he saw mine and he rescued me because I'm needed. But I don't understand what for.'

'Talib was wise Imari. He saw what you're capable of. Do you know why father chose your name?' He shook his head. 'Your name means faithful. He chose that name because of the first act you carried out in life. You sacrificed your first feed so Karamu could have it and become healthy and strong. That showed true compassion,' he looked at me in disbelief. 'You've displayed strength and love towards Karamu since her first breath. And you are the same with all of your friends. You have a beautiful spirit Imari, and Talib would have seen that. One day your fate will be written, and I feel your destiny will be great.'

Imari puffed out his chest and smiled. 'Will I be as great as you Berko? Or father?' I felt my face get warm at such a comparison and looked away a little as a tear bubbled up in my eye. 'Will I Berko?' he asked again.

I blinked hard and looked back at him. 'I really think you will be amazing Imari. Truly amazing,' his smile widened. 'But of course... you could never be as great as me Imari,' I smiled wryly, and then I shoved him playfully onto his side with my shoulder.

He giggled, and then jumped on top of me, tickling my ribs with his hoofs and laughing, 'admit it, I will be just as great.'

'Ok, ok... I give in. You will be the greatest wildebeest on the savannah. Oh master.' We both led there giggling for a while and then I turned back to look at him. 'I'm really proud of you Imari. And I'm truly blessed to have you as my brother.' I touched my cheek to his and he pressed his into mine. We both got up and walked slowly towards the herd and he said quietly 'I love you Berko.'

'I love you too.'

Imari ran over to Karamu and led next to her, pressing himself up to her lovingly and said 'I love having the best sister.' I smiled to myself as Ayana came over. I told her about my chat with Imari and she nudged me gently and said softly, 'I am so proud how you're always able to cheer your siblings up.' And then she kissed my cheek.

We went for a walk in dusks soothing light. 'We will soon be in the northern territory,' I said, a nervous ache of nausea building in my stomach. 'But I wish my journey with you was for an eternity Ayana... What Imari said about Talib reminded me of our talks back south. Talib always said that my fate was written from an early age too. And the love I had within my heart was what guided my spirits and helped forge my destiny. But all these years I never saw it.' I stopped walking and as she noticed I wasn't beside her, she stopped too. 'And I think it's because it wasn't me that summoned those spirits,' I said as I looked to the horizon.

She looked at me with confusion. 'What do you mean Berko?'

I looked right into her eyes and my nervousness disappeared immediately. 'It was the love I had for you that they could see... Every time I saw you, every time we spoke. My heart grew ever larger and my love so much stronger. I know I have always loved you Ayana. And I know I always will. You make me who I am, and I will always cherish that.'

'I've always loved you too Berko. That's why I only wanted to be with you after the rut.'

I pressed my cheek to hers and whispered softly. 'I never want to be apart from you again Ayana. You complete my soul...' I swallowed hard, not allowing that ache to return. 'Would you complete my destiny Ayana, by joining me in marriage?'

She kissed my cheek and then looked right into my eyes, tears welling up in hers. 'Of course I would Berko. I'd love nothing more,' she said with a break in her voice. I held her as tightly as I could and then we kissed again. We sat among the long grass and watched the clear night sky. And as the moon came up over the plains, I could feel my heart grow larger by the minute, and I could finally see my destiny unfolding in the stars.

The following morning, Ayana and I gathered our families together. 'Is everything ok?' said father. 'What is so urgent you had to bring us all away from the herd?'

'As you all know Ayana and I have been friends our entire lives. And more recently we have been much closer and have spent lots of time together. Well after the Rut, Ayana chose me and we confirmed our feelings for each other.'

'We have always known you two would be more than just friends. It doesn't take Idriis' powers to see that,' said Jelani.

'Father!' said Ayana with embarrassment. 'What Berko... What we wanted to say was Berko has asked if I would join him in marriage. We would like to follow in your hoofsteps and turn down the tradition of a harem, instead joining together and loving only one another for life.' They all stood staring at us, and we were waiting for somebody to speak. Then after a really long wait, they all ran over and hugged us both.

When they finally let us go, my siblings ran straight back to Ayana, Karamu joyfully screaming 'I'm so excited. Now I can spend even more time with you.' And Imari gave her the biggest squeeze of all, but then went a bit shy when he realised what he'd just done.

'Ayana, I know how much Berko means to you and I know how much he adores you. I couldn't be happier,' said Jelani and then he turned to my parents. 'I have always thought the world of you all, and to have Berko as an honorary son makes me happier than I could have ever imagined. Imamu, you are my dearest friend and I am honoured to be able to call you my family.' He went over to my father and hugged him and then hugged my mother.

'I am so happy you have chosen love over dominance Berko,' said father. 'It takes great spirit to follow your heart, and to show true loyalty to the one you love. I am truly proud of you my son.' He turned back to Jelani and hugged him again. 'And I am proud he found love in Ayana. You have both raised a wonderful daughter;

she is strong, loyal and beautiful. I am yet to find the traits she got from you Jelani,' he nudged him with his shoulder and they both laughed.

'We were thinking of having it officiated soon, when we reach the northern territory,' said Ayana.

'I can't think of a better place,' Jelani said. 'It is a very sacred area for the herd, so it will be perfect for such an important ceremony. It will be safe there too, and the grasses and water will be plentiful, so we could truly celebrate the coming together of our families.' My parents both agreed and Mbali went over to hug Jelani. The four of them bowed their heads to us in respect, and then my siblings seeing them did the same, before running over to give us both another hug. I looked at Ayana and smiled lovingly, it meant so much to have all this support from both of our families.

The herd began the trek north. The northern territory was almost in sight and we would reach it sometime the following day. The herd knew this and the pace they had been marching for the last week soon got faster. The idea of reaching the sacred lands had given them all focus and the pace has gone from a trot to a canter. Ayana and I went to help my siblings keep up, but they were now enjoying it. 'Does everyone know about your ceremony?' Karamu asked as she happily galloped alongside us. A slight wind picked up and rain began to fall. Usually this would put us off, but at the speed we'd been moving, it was nice to cool off.

The herd was due a rest stop, but the downpour allowed us to lick water from our lips as we ran. We occasionally checked on our friends to make sure they were all coping with the pace we were setting, but they said they were fine to continue. We were able to run much further than our friends the zebra, but they were too focused on the north to hold us back.

We finally made a rest stop two thirds of our usual distance. The leaders said we should break for longer to refuel, but the herd all wanted to push on. Ayana and I sat with my siblings and encouraged them to eat and drink so they could make the final section of the trip. They were so excited about the ceremony in the north that they wouldn't stop talking. 'Come on, both of you. You have to drink before we set off again.'

'You didn't answer me earlier Berko,' said Karamu. 'Are the others excited about the wedding as well? Is that why they're running?'

'The rest of the herd are excited about the north Karamu. They wouldn't care about our news. Besides, the ceremony is only going to be for our families,' I said.

'So is no one else coming?' She asked.

'Some of our closest friends might come to give their blessings, but it is for our families to come together as one, in support of our dedication. It isn't going to be like the ceremonies you have seen before.'

'Oh,' she said with disappointment.

'It will be way better than any of those Karamu,' said Imari. 'And you'll actually get to be a part of this one.'

'Really?' she said with excitement. Ayana went over and told her how she could help us plan it while we're making the final journey to the north and she was really excited and started to come up with ideas straight away. I turned to Imari and gestured to him that we leave them both talking; we headed to the other small stream to take a drink.

'Thank you Imari. I didn't realise Karamu would be so upset that it was a small ceremony.'

'That's ok Berko. She hasn't shut up about it since this morning. She's annoying. But it has kept her moving. So... I'd rather listen to her going on about that than have to keep getting her to run,' he said flippantly, trying to seem like he didn't really care for her feelings.

'You are a good brother to her Imari,' I said, and we both went back to drinking some water.

We were still marching north when the sun was beginning to drop below the horizon to our left. The leaders had to work hard to get the herd to finally stop. Although we were all exhausted, it was only when we all sat in the grass that we realised how much our legs were aching. And how empty our bellies really were.

The leaders from all of the droves had gathered together and wanted to make an announcement. You could sense tension over the herd. Everyone was clearly apprehensive of what they had to say. The herd started to gather, all squeezing in tightly to get as close to the leaders as they could. As always, there were mutterings from the groups of animals gathered, all speculating about the news. Most were fearful there had been attacks but many were saying the pace was probably too much for some of the herd. After a while Idriis called for peace so the leaders could speak to us all. He indicated for my father to approach and speak to the herd.

'We didn't mean to panic you all by calling a meeting at such short notice, but we all felt you deserved to be kept up to date,' said father.

The mutterings got a little louder.

'Hush please,' said Hekima. 'Please listen to what we have to say.'

'Thank you Hekima. You all did an amazing job today maintaining that pace and pushing on like you did. And you can rest assured it was not in vain. As you all know, the northern territory is in sight. We were aiming to be there by some time tomorrow, possibly close to sundown. But your efforts have paid you dividends. The territory will be reached far sooner. If we rest well tonight, and push on at first light, we should be in the sacred lands long before our first rest stop.' The herd erupted, cheering and jumping with happiness.

'Well done everyone,' shouted Idriis. 'You deserve the rewards the territory has to offer. Now go off and enjoy the evening.'

The herd started to file away in all directions talking about the north with real excitement. The atmosphere was so much better, and the sound of joy and laughter filled the air.

As we awoke with the rising sun, we were aching but excited to get moving so we could get to the sacred lands as soon as possible. Everyone rushed some breakfast, grabbing mouthfuls of drying grass to chew while they walked. There was little water in the area we'd stopped. The rains had not fallen here for a while and the herd were beginning to worry about the northern territory. The rains should have been ahead of us, soaking the land for our arrival. Seekers usually report of droughts to our leaders but there had been no communications over the last few days. The idea we could have pushed on this far and this quickly for nothing would be a huge blow for all of us.

There was no message from the leaders or from any seekers that there was reason to turn back and head for richer grazing, so we all pushed on at our same heightened pace. As we began to tire, we were starting to fall back. But the leaders tried to keep the front of the herd moving as before. A seeker came swooping back towards the herd, and relayed a message to Idriis. He slowed for a second and dropped behind my father and Jelani before turning to Afia and whispering something into her ear. She nodded to Idriis before she turned and bolted across the front of the herd at great speed.

I noticed the rising sun was moving across as we marched. The herd had gradually begun to turn to the right and were now on a north-easterly course. The leaders picked up the pace and the herd instinctively followed until we were once again galloping the final stretch of our journey

As the sun turned bright yellow, I could see something magical coming over the horizon. An oasis. And it was beckoning us towards it. The herd picked up speed and we were running as fast as we physically could. 'Not far now!' shouted Idriis, and the message was passed back through the herd like a gust of wind. My heart was pounding; the sound of my pulse blocked out all the other sounds around me. The bright pastures of the sacred land were gleaming, getting ever closer as we strode. Up ahead, the grasses were bright green, and glistening with dew. The meadow flowers were vibrant, and as numerous as the heavenly stars. There were trees dotted around the grasslands, rich with foliage which would provide food and shelter for many. All of the efforts we'd put into this trek were finally being rewarded, and there was plenty there for everyone.

7
The Sacred Territory

Our stay so far in the north had been incredible. The entire herd was relaxed and able to feed whenever we liked. There was plenty of water for all of us too, from a number of meandering streams running through the grasslands. We'd been free of our enemies for a while and the threat of attack was a second thought. And although the grief we suffered at the banks of the Mara was still deeply felt within our hearts, our stay up here would surely help. When you're able to relax, you focus on the most important things in your life, so the more time we had to remember our loved ones, the easier it would become to let go of our sorrow and reminisce on the times we all enjoyed together.

My time with Ayana had been amazing; we'd spent all of our days relaxing in the sun between the rain storms. We were really excited as our families had already arranged our ceremony with the elders. It was to be held in two days time, when the sun was at its highest. My father and Jelani had been spending time preparing the area for us. We weren't allowed to be involved at this stage as the ground needed to be cleared and the soil blessed by the elders, it was important the soil was clear of any vegetation so we could be grounded within the consecrated earth. So Ayana and I could merely observe as the preparations took place.

Watching them carry this out just for us was truly humbling, and it gave me such reassurance that our parents believed we had made the right choice. Spending the rest of my life with Ayana would make me so happy, and when I look at my parents and I see their devotion for one another, I know that is what I truly want with Ayana.

The wildebeest follow one of the two ancient traditions. We either use the rut to establish dominance and build a harem, siring many children with lots of different females. Or we mate for life with our one chosen love. This is extremely rare within our species; we are often bound by our instincts, so we base our lives around survival, which is why a harem helps our species grow. Pairing through love means we bear only one offspring each year, but the love we have for our partner is passed to our child in abundance. We choose our own lives in this world and we follow whichever tradition we want. And although what we've chosen is not commonly practiced by the wildebeest, I know it is right for me. I am choosing to follow my heart and joining my soul with Ayana's, and I want to show my true devotion, not just to her but to the entire herd.

Ayana was spending time with the females as it is customary for us to stay away from each other for the final day before our ceremony. Karamu kept telling me how much Ayana missed me and it was difficult not to go and find her, to just speak to her quietly away from the others, but I knew I couldn't. So I hung around with Imari to keep my mind off things. I asked if he'd like to play a game but he said he'd rather sit by one of the streams and talk. 'Are you ok Imari? You've been very quiet again recently,' I said.

'I keep having a strange dream Berko,' he said with tears in his eyes. 'I keep seeing Talib. And last night I saw him in the ceremonial circle where you and Ayana are getting joined tomorrow. I... it always feels so real...' He got upset so I comforted him.

'It's ok Imari. Dreams are your minds way of putting things in order. Sometimes you dream of those you've lost because they're still within your heart. Talib is in all our hearts. But he wouldn't want you to be sad for him Imari.'

'I... I know, I just miss him Berko,' he sniffed loudly. 'I've tried to be strong for Zarifa, and I know she's getting better all the time. She enjoys hearing the stories I have of her father. But when I talk about him, I always think of that day.' I pressed my cheek to his and he sniffed again. 'In my dreams I keep walking over and he touches his head to mine. Then he whispers in my ear... but I can never hear what he's saying, I just hear the river.'

'What happened is still very raw Imari, it affected us all. Just remember, you are never alone. If you have another bad dream, or you just need to talk about what happened, come and find me. I'll always have time for you Imari.' He hugged me and I kissed him on the cheek. 'Come on; let's have a game of Ampe. I'll be *it*.'

'How are you feeling Berko?' asked mother as he checked my mane. 'Father has gone to meet with the elders. They will be joining us shortly.'

'I feel nervous,' I said looking past her to try to see Ayana. Imari and Karamu ran over and told me it was time to go, and mother gave me a huge hug before walking on ahead.

I stood within the circle our fathers had prepared for us, waiting to catch sight of Ayana as she arrived, and my father pressed his shoulder against mine lovingly. 'Calm down son, you have no reason to be nervous.'

I smiled at him but I couldn't answer, my mouth was too dry and I was concentrating too hard on not collapsing in a heap of nerves.

Mbali came into view and was walking ahead of Ayana so I couldn't quite see her. As Ayana moved to the side, the sunlight shone on her face and she looked beautiful in the bright midday light. I couldn't wait to speak to her again.

The ceremony was very private and the two families decided who else may be present. Afia and her family were going to attend, and Shirika who we wished to represent Talib. She was touched by the invite and said he would be so proud of us both. Her daughter Zarifa was also attending and my siblings had been keeping her and Khola entertained while the ceremony was prepared. Idriis and Hekima had also been invited, as they are our closest friends among the elders. Idriis was going to lead the ceremony; he led the ceremonies for both our parents' weddings, so it was really nice to have him lead ours too.

Idriis gathered the guests together and the children fell into line. He quietly guided everyone where to stand, and found it really amusing as we all got tied up. Ayana and I stood facing each other within the circle and each of our families stood behind us. Idriis, stood to my right, began the ceremony.

'As the chosen elder of this herd, I call upon the spirits to bless Berko and Ayana. To join their souls in love and in life, so they may at last become one in the eyes of the spirits. I ask that the spirits come down. To be present among us. And to bear witness to the true devotion these two have for one another. Friends and loved ones begin the ceremony.'

My siblings and all of the guests entered the circle. Along with our parents, they formed an unbroken ring around Idriis, Ayana and I by holding of the tail of whoever was in front of them. They began to trot.

'This ring resembles your love; it has no beginning and it has no end,' Idriis gave everyone a nod and they began to speed up. 'Their increasing speed resembles your devotion to one another; the love you give will drive you forward, becoming ever more powerful as you move throughout this life together. The earth resembles your commitment to each other; the more you put upon it, the stronger it becomes.'

As they ran faster around us, the dust began to build. 'The spirits are now among us,' cried Idriis loudly. 'I ask that you give your blessing for the choice Ayana and Berko have made. And I ask that you carry the love of their one true soul. Take it up to the skies and set it among the stars where it will remain for all eternity, never to be broken and never to fall back upon the earth.'

The dust rose up on the wind and everyone began to slow. As they stopped they all turned in to face us and bowed their heads to show their respect.

As all of the other guests left the circle, my family now stood behind Ayana and her parents stood behind me to give their blessing.

'Now before these witnesses,' Idriis continued, 'I announce the coming together of the two families. Your bond will be as strong as the love your offspring show for each other. And as they are joined together as one, they can rely on your undying support.'

Our families all said together, 'on us they can rely' and they bowed, first to us and then to each other.

'Then it is with the greatest honour that I can announce you both as husband and wife. Your souls are now joined and your bond is now sacred for all eternity.'

The two families cheered and the guests joined in. Karamu, Zarifa and Khola were dancing with glee and even Imari got excited and joined them as they cheered along with the adults.

Idriis bowed one last time and the guests all followed his lead. As everyone left the circle, they touched their foreheads to Ayana and then to me and gave us loving wishes. Ayana and I then gave Idriis a hug and thanked him for such an incredible ceremony.

'I was honoured to be asked,' he said in return and he then touched our foreheads too.

After the ceremony, we all headed for an area within the curve of one of the streams where we celebrated our marriage by partying long into the night. Our parents all told stories of our childhood and gave speeches, trying their hardest to embarrass us both. Jelani and Mbali welcomed me to their family as did my family with Ayana. We all had a feast of lush grass and the sweetest meadow flowers collected by Karamu, and we washed it all down with the coldest and purest water on the plains. My siblings had fun playing with Zarifa and Khola, and they were all allowed to stay up as long as they wanted. It was long after sundown when we finally made our way back to the join the rest of the herd.

During one of the leaders' meetings, our marriage was announced to the herd along with those of a number of other couples. So while we walked around, we would occasionally get congratulated by members of the herd who wanted to give their blessings for our choice. It makes me feel very mature when the older wildebeest come and speak to me about Ayana, they seem to take me much more seriously now than they ever did before.

In the meeting, the leaders made an announcement about the territory. We were to stay here for 90 days before heading slowly to the east of the sacred lands. This was very welcome news for the herd who could really relax and settle into the area. It was reported that the rains seemed set to remain for much of that time, keeping the grasslands saturated and maintaining a good supply of feed. The grasses were plentiful and there was more than enough for all of us, as long as we followed our strategy and kept rotating our grazing around the plains. The rains were also keeping the many streams flowing clear and cold. It was easy to see why this area was so sacred to our ancestors, and why it is still such a draw for us to this day.

The atmosphere in this Eden had been wonderful. We had been here for thirty days. The rains had fallen once or twice every day and the ground was soft and comfortable under hoof. When the rains were not falling, the sun was bright. The clouds seemed to vanish as quickly as they came and the herd was enjoying the opportunity to relax and bathe in the suns warming rays. Our morale had never been better. The entire herd had been happy and there had been celebrations and games most evenings. We had made new friends and forged new relationships as the droves came together and mingled as one more than ever.

Ayana and I walked in the midday sun to take a drink from one of the streams. We had been so happy since our ceremony and were discussing our plans for the future. When we reached the stream, Ayana turned to me and spoke softly, 'Berko, after the rut you chose to ignore all the other females and follow your heart. You chose to tell me the feelings you had for me and I told you I wanted only you. And then we went to the meadows and we confirmed our true love.

'Yes. It was a magical moment. One I would never have wanted to share with any other Ayana.'

'And I feel exactly the same...' she paused for a while and then took a deep breath. 'Well...'

'Is everything ok Ayana? You are starting to scare me.'

'That moment within the meadow Berko. You are going to be a father. We're going to be parents when we reach the sacred lands to the south.'

I looked at her with wide eyes, and I can only imagine a dopey expression on my face, 'really? Parents Ayana?' she nodded gently. My heart was pounding and my head fuzzy. I had to sit by the side of the stream. 'This is so exciting. How long have you known?'

'Not long, your mother noticed the signs. When she asked if I was ok about it, I told her how you are with your siblings. I know you will be an incredible father

Berko. And I am so happy to be spending my life with only you.' She sat down beside me and I kissed her gently.

'Ayana, with you as a mother, our child will be perfect. And you've made me the happiest wildebeest on these plains.'

We led in the warm sun bathed grass by the streams' curved bank and talked further about our future, only this time our plans had real purpose.

It was hard to believe, but 60 days had already passed. We had really been at peace since we arrived and the herd had been enjoying these blessed lands, just as our ancestors always intended. There was fresh grass and sweet meadow flowers for everyone, and an unending supply of clean cold water. The plains seemed to stretch on forever, and many of the herd were truly making the most of the open space, spreading far and wide throughout the land, only joining up again for official meetings. There was a good feeling through the herd, like the spirits were providing for us and truly rewarding our efforts for getting up here.

Some of our enemies were spotted in the area, and there were a number of attacks a few weeks ago, but it was still not enough to make us fear the area; it just meant we had to be more vigilant when walking around the outskirts of the territory. Our presence was likely to draw more of our enemies over time, but we were still relaxed and able to enjoy our stay on the sacred plains.

Since Ayana told me the incredible news that she's in calf, I'd been beaming with joy. At first I was taken aback, maybe even terrified at the thought of being a father, though I didn't let her know that of course. But the tranquillity of the sacred plains let me contemplate the important things in my life. Before we got up here, I couldn't see myself as mature, not mature enough to be a father at least. But I've learnt to put others before myself, and even to give guidance to my siblings and the other youngsters. I've shown I can lead alongside my father and make decisions that can aid others around me. And then of course there is Ayana. I chose to devote myself to her. I've loved her all my life and I know I want to spend the rest of my life with her. So if I can be mature enough to do all of this, surely I should be able to step up to fatherhood.

My siblings benefited more than most of us from being in the north. The rich grasses helped with their growth spurts and built their strength, so they'd have no trouble keeping up with the herd when we journey south. Imari had done really well to overcome the tragedy at the river. He'd been spending more time with Talib's daughter, Zarifa, and they'd helped each other through the grief they were feeling. Zarifa was really struggling with the loss of her father, so Imari told her more of the stories our parents told us about Talib, and she loved how close it made her feel to her father again. The happier Zarifa becomes, the stronger it makes Imari. Since coming north, they hung out together most days and their friendship was getting stronger all the time.

Karamu found it difficult to see her brother spending more time with his new friend than he did with her. When Ayana spoke to her, Karamu said it was more because Zarifa was her friend too, and she felt like they were pushing her out. Ayana explained Imari's reasons and Karamu realised he was just being typical Imari, putting everyone else first. After a few more days, I spoke to Imari about Karamu's feelings and he invited her along for their next meet up. Now the three of them are inseparable. It's really great to see such an amazing thing come out of such awful circumstances. And since their misunderstanding, Imari and Karamu are stronger than ever too. Whenever he wasn't spending time with his new friend, he was concentrating on his bond with his sister.

Ayana was going with our mothers to meet with some of the other females. All of the pregnant females have been bonding and learning from their elders about what to expect. Whenever I asked about it she told me it's sacred between the females, so I knew to just leave them all to it. While she was off with the others, I spent time with the leaders. I was still keen to learn as much as I could from my father, especially now I will have my own child to teach. The leaders reduced their duties while we stayed up here as it was much safer, so there was less need to be so watchful throughout the days. They still took turns carrying out head counts and walking the perimeter twice a day, and they still met up regularly to report and plan the next stages. But most of their time together was social.

Karamu and Zarifa were invited along with Ayana to meet some of the females in the nursing group. Some of them had daughters the same age as Karamu, and thought it would be nice for them to go and play while the adults met up to talk. Imari was invited along, but he couldn't stand to be around all those girls while they talked about babies. I took him off for the afternoon to teach him some of the things father had taught me. He was quite excited because I took him further from the herd than he can usually go.

After our lesson we went for a run in the pastures before finding a stream to sit by to get a drink. 'Thank you Berko, I've had a good time today,' he said as he gulped some water from the stream.

'We don't get to do this enough Imari. I thought you might like the break.'

'Yeah, it's been fun.' He went back for another gulp. 'I had more dreams Berko,' he said, water dripping down his chin.

'Not bad dreams again I hope?'

'No,' he wiped his chin on his front leg. 'The same ones. About Talib,' he said happily. 'But I heard what he said this time. When he whispered in my ear he said "thank you for looking out for her, I knew you would make me proud." Do you think it means he's happy I've been helping Zarifa?'

'I'm sure he'd be very proud of you Imari, I know I am. You have shown real maturity recently. You are a wonderful young wildebeest.'

'Thank you Berko,' he said before having more water.

8
Trekking South

There was a feeling of sadness over the herd. Our time in the sacred lands was finally coming to an end and although everyone knew it was necessary to go, it wasn't easy to leave everything behind. The leaders called their final meeting at sunset the night before to announce the plan to journey south. The rains up here had been absent for a while and storms had been spotted on the horizon, which we must follow if we want to flourish. Our time in the area won't be forgotten anytime soon. And although we knew we'd be back again, it was still sad to be leaving.

For the next one hundred days, we'd be travelling south, following the rains as they lead us back towards the birthing grounds. Back to where it all began. The journey would take us once again across the Mara, albeit on a narrower part, but the dangers it holds still bring us anxiety. We would be trekking almost continually, and even when we have the occasional break, it'd never compare to our time up here. The rains would provide us the grass we need to keep going, but we'd have to wait until the south to see pastures like these again.

The herd was making the most of the luscious grass, and even when they were full, they kept chewing on mouthfuls of grass, just to savour the taste. The water in these streams was so cold and fresh, that it would be hard to find anything that compared when we leave.

But it was the anticipation that was worst of all. We were all waiting for the message to come through the herd, telling us to begin our trek. The leaders kept having deep discussions to decide when we would move out, but they were usually very candid at risk of the herd leaving before time. We tried to keep up the feeling of calm, but whenever one leader approached another, it was hard not to expect an announcement.

A seeker came swooping over the herd to Idriis with some news. She came from the east and looked worried. Idriis talked to the others before approaching the herd to relay the message.

'Everyone. It is time. There is news that some of our enemies have learnt we were in these lands. They have tracked our scent and are getting too close for us to ignore. Some packs of hyenas have attempted to attack the herd during the night. If they have found us, then our other enemies will not be too far behind. I know you have all been very happy here, but fate has made its decision. Make sure you have all eaten and had plenty to drink before we embark on the journey.'

The leaders of each drove split up and headed off to round up their groups. The herd panicked and rushed to the best grazing areas to grab one last mouthful of the grass they'll miss so much. The calmness that had lay over the herd for so long was evaporating with the morning dew, but it was the fear of losing this pasture and what it represents, rather than being hunted by our enemies that was causing such commotion. When we begin our trek, we'll no longer have the freedom that made us all so happy, but will once again become slaves to our instincts and follow as the herd we are. We rely on the rains to tell us where to go, and the guidance from the leaders to take us to prosperous land. And although this gives us safety and purpose, it is sad to have to stop thinking for ourselves again.

While the herd made their final preparations for the journey, my father asked if I'd come and join him and the other leaders. When I got there, Idriis welcomed me as he always does and said he wants to ask something of me.

'You showed true courage and initiative back at the Mara Berko,' he said. 'To come to the aid of the herd in a time like that shows a level of loyalty that is seldom seen among the herd. We would like to have you by our sides for the crossing south. If you would do us the honour of course?'

I was stunned, but it meant so much to be asked by Idriis. 'I would love to help, I know the crossing is a difficult time for us all, and without Talib it is going to be a much bigger challenge... so yes, I'd like to be there to assist where I can. Although... I do ask that I can see Ayana across safely. If that is ok?'

'Of course Berko. I know you wouldn't want anything happening to her. Especially now,' said Idriis.

'I didn't realise you all knew? Did my mother tell you she is with calf?'

My father's eyes widened and he beamed with a huge smile. 'You are going to be a father Berko?' he said excitedly.

'Is that not what Idriis meant?' I said sheepishly.

'I just assumed you would want to protect her now you are married... But this is fantastic news,' Idriis replied joyfully, 'I think you will make a wonderful father.'

'I'm going to be a grandfather,' said my father in a state of shock as the reality of it truly sunk in, and he looked over at Jelani who was just as stunned as he was. He came and hugged me tightly and then Jelani came over and hugged us both.

'I am so happy for you Berko,' Jelani said, and he and father both looked at each other with large grins and then touched cheeks.

Idriis came and touched his forehead to mine, 'I am really proud of you too Berko, and make sure you give my love to Ayana for me.'

'Of course I will Idriis.'

Father and Jelani were still laughing with shock and excitement so I coughed loudly. 'Sorry Idriis,' said Jelani, still smiling proudly. 'Please continue.'

'Right... Oh yes,' he smiled. 'Well. It will be the same as our northerly crossing,' he continued, trying to recall what he'd been saying before. 'We will assess the best spot and go from there. I suggest you split your time between the sides then Berko. When Ayana arrives, you can enter the water and see her across to safety. Then resume your duties on the south bank.'

I agreed with the plan and then we all discussed the finer details of the crossing and worked out the roles we would all play. And every now and then my father looked over at me and smiled broadly.

I wanted to tell Ayana immediately and make sure she didn't mind me leaving her to go and help the leaders.

It isn't fair to make that type of decision without her when it affects her so massively.

'Of course you should help Berko,' she said when I explained everything. 'You are maturing quickly, and it's clear that Idriis has a lot of trust in you. The crossing is dangerous whether you assist or not, but with you keeping watch, I'd feel much safer, you know that,' she touched her cheek to mine. 'I know you are going to be a father, and we are now married, but you can't let that hold you back from following your fate. I am a part of your story now, and our calf will be too. But you can't let that stop you from doing anything. Besides, I'll be fine, and I'll have enough assistance from both our families.'

'I have asked to see you to safety Ayana. When you arrive at the river, I'm going to join you and help you make the crossing. I can resume my duties on the other side.'

'Thank you. You are a great husband Berko. I can see why Idriis trusts you so much.'

I met with the leaders to assess the river for the crossing, but all the way there they kept saying how eerily quiet the Mara was. On our arrival, the river had stopped flowing all together; the muddy bank was dry and the riverbed full of jagged rocks. Father whispered to Idriis that he saw some movement among the rocks, and as we edged a little closer, they were undulating slowly.

Idriis indicated for us all to be silent and then he kicked a clump of dry dirt out into the middle of the riverbed. As it hit the sundried crust and broke into a dusty cloud, the river growled and rumbled. The sound radiated out from the centre until all of the rocks were joining in this harrowing chorus.

The river was completely full of crocodiles, all anticipating our return. They knew we couldn't fight our instincts to follow the storms back south, and as our route remains almost unchanged, they'd all squeezed into the stretch of river that provided us with the best crossing point we could find for miles. They must have been waiting there for a while, because the mud and silt on their scaly backs had completely dried out under the heat of the sun.

We all edged back out of sight and the leaders all spoke in hushed tones to avoid alerting them to our presence. As we walked along the high bank, the leaders tried to work out where the herd could all cross safely. But the crocodiles had filled the entire river; they stretched from one bank to the other and we could see them all the way to the next curve.

We carried on a little further but as far as we walked the river was still the same. I'd never seen so many of our enemies in one place at once. Our crossing looked impossible, and with our other enemies now trailing our scent from the sacred plains, our fate didn't look good.

Idriis' booming voice split through the silence as he called to us all from one of the highest parts of the bank, 'This is perfect. Come and look everyone. This will allow even the youngest among the herd to get across safely.'

I looked at my father, thinking Idriis had lost it, and he looked at me with just as much confusion. But just as we were going to meet him, there was the unmistakable sound of rumbling. We all stood back from the bank as the sound of cracking mud filled the air, followed by the squelching and clawing of wet silt as the crocodiles awoke from their slumber. All of the crocodiles were scrambling through the mud to follow the sound of Idriis' booming voice; their minds focused solely on their next possible meal. They piled one on top of the other to sit in wait below our feet, and as they vied for the best position, they growled and snapped their jaws to warn one another off of their patch.

Idriis signalled to us to head off, and we silently walked away from the river's edge. 'I didn't think they would fall for that so easily,' he said. 'We need to gather the herd as quickly as we can, I don't know how long it will take them to realise we fooled them. Jelani and Afia, could you both head back to the original crossing point so the herd know where to head? The number of crocodiles that have headed this way should mean that area is safer; I think it will be our best crossing point. The rest of us will go back and round up the herd.' Jelani and Afia agreed and headed off as quietly as possible. When the rest of us were far enough from the river, we galloped towards the herd as fast as we could.

'Everyone, it is time,' yelled Idriis, and the herd all looked up as one. 'We have to make the crossing now. We cannot turn back this time. Make sure you are all fully prepared.'

The herd started to head over and followed the leaders back to the river. When we approached our original crossing point, Jelani and Afia came to meet us, 'most of the crocodiles have moved,' said Afia.

'Your idea worked Idriis, the numbers are down considerably. There are still some who must have read your tactics, but it is far less overwhelming than before,' said Jelani.

Father, Idriis and Afia, made the crossing first to keep watch from the other side. They were careful to avoid the thrashing and swirling of the crocodiles as they went. When they signalled back to us, the herd built up along the north bank and the remaining crocodile's eyes widened with glee. We had all been feasting well during our stay in the northern territory, and this was clearly visible to the crocodiles.

When the number of wildebeest, gazelle and zebra was again critical along the bank, we had to start our crossing. The flow of the river was much slower this time, but the amount it frothed and swirled was far worse. As the herd bounded into the river, the crocodiles became ferocious. They leapt and thrashed at the slightest movement in the water and got tangled on themselves as they lashed out for a kill.

The herd were in a state of panic, jumping clear of the water's surface, almost flying above it with fear. The adults were causing a huge distraction, their large healthy bodies too tempting a meal for the crocodiles to resist. The young among the herd, now knowing what to look for, found it easier to make the crossing, and the energy they'd gained from the grasses in the north helped them move more quickly through the water. A wildebeest vanished beneath the surface and the screams of those nearest to him echoed up the river.

When Ayana arrived, I took the opportunity to join her. While she trudged through the deep sticky mud of the bank, I guarded her, kicking the muzzle of a large crocodile who tried to creep up on us both from the murky shallows. In her panic, she slipped and fell as the bank dropped away under hoof, but she soon regained her balance as she felt for the bottom.

On the other bank, I helped Ayana to the safety of my mother and Mbali's grasp and then I rejoined the leaders to assist in the efforts. Imari took it upon himself to help Karamu and Zarifa across. Pushing them forward with his shoulder, and lashing out at the enemies around them, kicking mud into their faces to hinder their attack. The leaders watched him closely from the bank and Idriis said quietly to father that he shows true potential.

We helped everyone to safety and counted the injured among those resting in the sun. Despite the numbers of our enemies and their thirst for our blood, the crossing went fairly smoothly. The furore in the water actually helped us, as the more the crocodiles fought with each other, the less success they had in catching a meal.

As the last of our drove arrived at the bank, we could see a tsunami of scaly bodies pouring down stream. Jelani ran to warn the next drove of the danger and they quickly changed course. They headed down stream to cross at our decoy site as most of the crocodiles were now heading our way.

Jelani galloped back to the river and without checking, he leapt right into the middle of the current and disappeared beneath a sea of crocodiles. Ayana and Mbali watched in terror at the frenzy within the water, the creatures were twisting and thrashing in the muddy soup. Ayana screamed and tried to get to the edge of the bank, but Mbali held her back as red froth bubbled to the surface. There was a long silence as everything stood still, Ayana's sobs muffled by my racing pulse inside my head.

Jelani finally broke through the water as he came up for air nearer to us. He used every bit of energy he had left to charge though the water and drag himself over the mud of the bank. Among the frenzy, an injured crocodile roared in agony as he fought to get away, only to be dragged straight back into the furore. My mind came rushing back from the slow fuzz as father asked me to help him drag Jelani to dry land. Jelani fell exhausted into the grass to catch his breath. And Mbali and Ayana threw themselves on top of him, suffocating him further with their love.

With the abundance of enemies in the water, the leaders didn't want to hang around. There could be more of our enemies lurking in the grasses around us, so they got the herd moving quickly. Heading south away from the river we marched until our legs were throbbing with exhaustion, and as we found an area rich in lush grass, we were given a rest stop. We were able to relax for the rest of the day.

The sky darkened with the lowering sun and Idriis called a meeting. The herd gathered slowly around the leaders, still feeling the effects of the crossing in our legs.

'Well done to you all for making such an efficient crossing today, despite the obvious dangers we came across,' Idriis said to the herd. 'It is however with deep sadness I have to report a small number of losses. I think it is only right that we carry out the traditional ceremony to mark our respects for our fallen.' The herd lowered their heads in sympathy and the leaders began the ceremony.

When the meeting was adjourned and the ceremony complete, we all sat and contemplated the memory of those we'd lost. And through the sadness we had felt and the starkness of the reality, we finally saw our path being forged. Now we have made it safely across the Mara, the journey will be easier and we can all look forward to the southern lands once again.

9
Homeward Bound

The signs of Mvuli had shown themselves on the horizon. The scent of rain was on the breeze and the lightning in the distance looked fruitful. Mvuli is the short rainy period that we all rely on so deeply. It prepares the grass for us, making it rich in the nutrients the females need for the sacred southern lands. These nutrients are passed to their unborn calves to ensure they are healthy and strong enough to stand soon after they are born.

The dry season started just before we left the sacred northern territory, so the prospect of heavy rains was exciting for us all. The rain fell occasionally at the beginning of our stay in the north, and for a couple of days at the start of our journey south. This created surface water on the plains for us all to drink. But the rains had definitely left us now. We hadn't seen any rainfall for a few days, or even the hint of a cloud, and the heat was becoming unbearable for some of our friends. We wildebeest were still managing well under the heat of the sun, but decided to take longer rest stops so our friends could recover. The elders of the zebra said we could continue without them; they would catch up when the temperature dropped with the sun. But we couldn't do that. We always travel as a herd, so it goes against our better judgement to leave others behind because they're struggling.

The breaks were allowing us to rest and we'd been travelling further when the sun went down. We'd been making good ground at dusk to keep on schedule. This was helping the young and old keep up with the rest of us and our friends had told us how much they appreciated it. They respected us for deciding to stay with them instead of going on ahead.

We were all glad we didn't go on without them, but I think Imari was the most relieved. He has really taken it upon himself to look out for Zarifa, and believes his dream was a message from Talib. Their friendship just keeps getting stronger and he has begun to mature because of it.

When I look at both of my siblings, I often forget they were born only minutes apart. Karamu still has that sweet innocence that I adore in her. She is always asking questions and is so excited by the answer you give her, always happy to have learned something new. But Imari is becoming much more mature. He already shows true intelligence and can hold a clever conversation. And he has a very protective nature, looking out for those around him and making sure they are ok. I'll admit, he can still be a little evasive if you try to talk to him about anything he finds embarrassing, but then he is still young. It's just really hard to remember that sometimes.

The heat was becoming difficult even for us. Today we couldn't even see the horizon. Pools of water sat ahead of us, reflecting the sky on its surface. The leaders started to discuss the route, fearing we'd turned off course and were heading for one of the many lakes. They decided to push on and we remained on course, but we never came across those lakes we could see.

Walking through the dry plains, the long grasses were whipping our shins and scratching our legs. The zebra tried to eat some of it on the hoof to boost their energy, but it was too dry even for them. The more we walked, the dustier it became, and at one point we had to take a break just to allow the dust to settle. It was getting in our eyes and throats and was making the journey too difficult.

Sat on the hard ground, with the dry grasses poking our skin made the rest stop more tedious than the journey itself. We usually relish these times, but now we just wanted to get moving again. But the heat made that impossible so we were forced to rest and wait for the sun to pass overhead. None of the herd could muster the energy to talk to each other, even the leaders lay there in silence.

As I lay next to Ayana, I was listening to the song of the savannah. The insects flying around us and the swishing of tails attempting to hit them away, the occasional huff from one of the animals in the herd. The lightest of breezes rustled the grass and disturbed the chirping of the crickets for the slightest of moments. Then in the distance was a light rumble of thunder. It seemed to go on for ages, and it perked us up quicker than finding the green pastures of the north. The herd all sat up as one and watched towards the horizon, ears pointed in the direction of the storm. Another rumble echoed across the hazy air and the herd all stood up, mesmerised by its call. Nobody spoke, but we all just looked to the leaders. They gave a light smile and raised their heads in the direction of the storm, and we all began following slowly, but with real purpose once more.

CHASING THE RAIN

We endured the long hot days, hoping in our hearts we would soon be rewarded by the spirits for never giving up. On the hottest day, as we aimed for the horizon and chased the sound of the thunder, a strange mass appeared in the distance. The closer we got, the larger it became and it was moving in different directions. We all slowed as the leaders got more wary. We couldn't risk walking into enemy territory when we had such little energy to escape. Idriis sent one of the seekers ahead to report what they saw and we all stood completely still awaiting the news. When he returned, he was laughing.

'What is it Macaria?' asked Idriis.

'It is our friends retuning from the west Sir. It is the Eland back to meet with us again.'

The animals at the front of the herd had listened to what was said and the message soon made it back to the others. The news gave us all a massive burst of energy and we started towards the mass on the horizon with joy in our hearts.

As we marched across the plain, the sky darkened. A rumble of thunder exploded above us and the rains fell heavily to the ground. The relief was immeasurable. The cool drops of rain saturated our coats and we licked the streams of water running down our faces. As we neared the mass of eland, Kwame came to the edge of the troop. 'I see you brought the rains with you. I couldn't have wished for a better gift,' he said joyfully.

As we all mingled with the eland and they caught up with their friends among the herd, Kwame came over to greet father and Jelani properly. 'It is so good to see you all again. No Talib? Where is the old boy? I thought he would be leading you all.'

Father touched cheeks with Kwame and whispered the news of Talib to him. Kwame folded at the knees as he took it in, and then bowed in his memory. 'He has created a vast void in this herd Kwame. One that will never be filled again,' said father and he bowed too.

The rains lasted for a long time, soaking the ground and creating great pools of water we were able to drink from. The stars had brought our good friends back safely, and provided us with plenty of water for our wonderful celebrations.

The celebrations went long into the night and the atmosphere was incredible. The rains had cooled the earth, so as the evening came down it was comfortable to sit and talk and laugh.

Father and Jelani invited Kwame and his family to come and join us for a while. We shared stories from our time in the north and the eland told us all about the west.

'The great lake was our saviour since the last time we saw you,' Kwame told us. 'The heat had been too much for the troop so we had to rest at the shores of the lake for much of the time. Thankfully our dear friends the buffalo offered us the warmest reception, and there was ample grass and vegetation for us all on the soil around the lake. Our time there was good; we were able to relax in preparation for our journey here.'

'I am so happy to see you have returned to us safely,' said father, 'I always worry when our herd breaks apart like that.'

'The lake, despite the life it gives, was dangerous, but we were good at avoiding the enemy so there were few incidents. We chose a good area where we could all stay that provided us with the safety and the supply of food we all needed. We were lucky not to have to tempt fate,' he lowered his head. 'I cannot believe Talib is gone.'

'The loss of Talib will never leave me, but the gift he provided in saving my son will never be forgotten,' said father. 'The northern territory was the herd's saviour. We are a large herd but the area provided many riches. But, as you said, we had to tempt fate in order to get there. It was just the worst price to pay for our salvation.'

Silence hung over the families as we all remembered Talib, so Jelani nudged Kwame playfully to break the tension. 'You haven't heard the best news of all Kwame. Berko and Ayana are now married.'

'Wow, congratulations. I wondered how long it would take you both to tell each other how you felt.'

My face got hot and Ayana placed her head on my shoulder to hide her embarrassment.

'We held the ceremony in the north. And best of all, we are going to be grandparents too,' said father.

'That is fantastic news,' Kwame said excitedly. 'I haven't seen a match this perfect since both of your parents. It is rare to see such love and devotion in the wildebeest, but when it happens, it is truly wonderful to see. I am so happy for the two of you,' he bowed his head to us both and then looked up again. 'To Ayana and Berko, and the life they are bringing to this herd.'

The others all bowed in response and hailed the toast.

'Our daughter, Hadiya, met a young male when they were at the lakeside,' Kwame then continued.

'Father?' Hadiya said with embarrassment.

'He stood up for her against a territorial male hippo of all things, a real beast too. She was in awe. They have been inseparable ever since. I think this is the first time you've been apart isn't it?' Hadiya squirmed with humiliation. 'Sorry sweetie. But seriously, he is a great young eland. He reminds me of you Berko.' Again I felt my face get hot, I couldn't think of any type of response. 'I am very proud of you Hadiya.'

'Thanks?' she said quietly, but I knew exactly how she felt.

'Ok, so let's catch up on the other events shall we?' said Binah, trying to steer the conversation away from us. She could see he'd embarrassed most of the youngsters and she felt sorry for us.

Ayana and I asked Hadiya if she wanted to go and have a catch up, and let our parents have a more grown up chat. So we took my siblings and Kinuka away and the six of us went to the open plains. My siblings and Kinuka played Ampe while Hadiya, Ayana and I sat in the long grass to watch the stars, and give our faces time to cool off.

The following morning there was a heavy mist over the herd. The rising sun was bringing the temperature up quickly and the water on the ground was lifting like clouds from the earth. The moisture made the temperature even higher and the air was so thick it was difficult to breath.

The leaders met up to discuss the plan for the morning. The air would make travelling hard for us all, especially the older generation, so it was decided we'd hold off until the mist had lifted. This was welcome news for many who were suffering after staying up so late, partying with the eland.

The leaders called upon the seekers and asked that they keep a watchful eye over the herd until the mist had dispersed. We all took the opportunity to fill our stomachs with fresh grass and drink from the remaining pools of water left on the plain before they'd evaporated like all the rest. The peaceful morning also gave us more time to catch up with our friends.

As the temperature rose, we all began to feel extremely relaxed and once more at ease with the thought of carrying on. The seekers were darting around overhead and whistling their call, so it was clear that the leaders were thinking about us moving again soon.

A message came through the herd that the mist was clearing to the south so it would be best to start moving if we were to make any kind of headway today. Idriis and the other leaders called for the herd to follow and they led us off through the thick white swirl of cloud. The light was getting a little brighter as the mist was burning off, and the heat of the sun was finally reaching our bodies. Looking back through the herd, it looked smaller than it had ever seemed before, many of the animals still hidden deep inside the vapour on the air.

The leaders set a slow, easy pace the herd would be able to manage in the humid conditions. Ayana and I stayed back with my siblings to take the pressure off our mothers after their late night with the eland. I was telling Karamu about the Mist and why it forms on the hot mornings when it had rained. I always love telling her new things and seeing the interest in her eyes.

The herd surged forward, almost tripping us. 'What's happening Berko?' asked Karamu, a little scared.

'It must be the poor visibility of the mist Karamu. The herd are probably unable to see how fast we are moving ahead of them.'

There was another large push as the herd thrust forward, followed by mass panic. The air filled with the sound of screams and heavy hoofsteps as the herd parted, and animals charged left and right. Karamu was separated from the rest of us as the panicked herd started to spread out in all directions.

In the vast clearing made by the herd, three lionesses came skulking out through some thick grass and lunged towards Karamu. Mother ran to get between her and one of the lionesses, but in the confusion, my sister ran to get away. Seeing her sparked the lioness's instinct to give chase and she sprinted after Karamu.

Imari and I gave chase to try to catch up and help her. She was running as fast as her legs would carry her and my brother was quickly gaining on them. Imari was reading his sisters every move and when she turned tightly in the dirt and doubled back, Imari took his chance and charged at the lioness. His tiny horns caught her front leg and sent her spilling onto the ground, her head hitting the floor and her body rolling right over the top.

In her anger, she quickly leapt up and gave chase to Imari. I got to Karamu, but she told me to go and help Imari. The lioness chased my brother. As he tried to turn she lashed at him, hooking her claws into the flesh of his shoulder, bringing him down into the dirt. He cried out in agony as she pulled herself up and swung her other paw over his neck in one fluid move. She grabbed his other shoulder and pinned him to the ground. As I got nearer to them I saw her grab for his neck with her teeth. But as she tried to bite down on his throat, I rammed my horns into her ribs, pushing her over. Her focus wasn't broken and her thirst for blood was far too strong, so she just gripped Imari even tighter and rolled right over, pinning him to the floor again. I took a step back and forced my horns harder into her side, tearing her flesh with a nauseating rip. The lioness screamed in agony, letting go of Imari. With a heavy turn of my head, I lifted the lioness up with my horns within her ribs, and threw her to the ground with a thud. In her anger, she turned towards me, 'run Imari,' I cried as he quickly got to his hoofs and ran towards my mother and Mbali.

The lioness lashed out at me, catching my muzzle with her paw and cutting my face. I stumbled backwards and tripped, falling onto my back.

Before I could even move out of the way, she lunged towards me again, her sharp claws aiming right for my neck. But as she stretched out her paws, the large tear in her side opened up and she fell into the dirt, letting out a piercing high pitched scream of agony. I backed away slowly, not taking my eyes off her as she struggled to her paws. Defeated, she limped slowly towards some long grass in the distance and dropped down heavily to lick her wounds.

Ayana had gathered Karamu after her fright and they both went and hugged Imari to thank him for what he had done. Then they all came over and leapt on top of me in sheer relief and Karamu thanked me for saving Imari. Imari gave me a huge hug too. 'Thank you Berko,' he said, 'you saved my life.'

'You saved Karamu's. You were amazing Imari. And I'm so glad you are ok.'

The leaders had heard what happened and turned back to help as quickly as they could. 'Are you all ok?' panted Father as he arrived.

'We are fine Imamu,' said mother. 'Your sons saved Karamu.' When Mother and Mbali explained to the leaders what had actually happened, my father came over and gave the three of us a large, loving hug. 'Thank the stars you are all safe,' he said, and hugged us again even tighter.

The other two lionesses had charged into the crowd further back and separated another youngster from the herd. They forced him out into the open plains and his mother gave chase to try to help him. One of the lionesses turned her attention on the mother and she was caught. Some of the other animals managed to get the youngster to safety and protect him while the pair of lionesses carried off their quarry.

The leaders gathered the herd to check everyone was ok. They said the herd should head for the Nusu Woodlands on the horizon; the giraffe and the rhinos could help keep us safe. So we all picked up the pace, despite the heat, and aimed to reach the destination before sundown. If the lionesses have drawn attention to their success, then we would be at a greater risk of attack from our other enemies, so we had to move on to the woodlands as quickly as possible.

When we arrived at the woodlands, our friends were overjoyed to see us all again. It was great to catch up with them all and there were even some of our friends that the herd hadn't seen since we passed through last year. The Rhinos were telling us that some of our enemies had tried to come through the woodlands recently, but they managed to scare them away for good. With so much help from them all, we'd be able to stay here and relax until morning.

Mbali came over and spoke to my mother and father; she was worried about the youngster involved in the attack. 'I have spoken to Jelani and he says the child has no family to help him Imamu?'

'No, unfortunately he was born to a new mother during the last birthing season. She was one of a harem, but she had no other family to speak of. He is currently being looked after by of one of the elders until we leave the woodlands, but he is the same age as Karamu and Imari, so she is finding it very difficult to cope.'

'I would like to help Imamu, if that is ok? I couldn't bear to see a youngster go through such a devastating ordeal and have nobody to look after him. And I would be able to take care of him on a permanent basis.'

'That is very honourable Mbali. Are you sure you would want to take that responsibility on?'

'I am certain. I have always wanted more children, but as you know I have been too afraid to calf again after Ayana's birth,' my mother touched her cheek to Mbali's. 'I have so much love to give and I feel I would be able to offer him the support he needs at this difficult time.'

'I think you would be perfect Mbali,' said mother. 'And he would certainly benefit from having stability at this time. He is far too young to cope on his own.'

'I agree,' said father. 'I will go and speak with the elders, I am sure they would agree too. I will report back to you as soon as possible Mbali,' he said, and pressed his cheek to hers softly.

'Thank you Imamu. I look forward to what they have to say.'

In the shelter of the woodlands, the herd felt safe. The elephants and rhinos offered us protection and ensured we could all get a good amount of rest before the morning, and the giraffe told the leaders they'd keep a close eye on the horizon for us all. The herd was shaken by today's attack so being here with our good friends made it much easier to calm down. My siblings were still finding it difficult to relax after what had happened, so Ayana and I sat with them for a while. We tried to keep their minds off it by making jokes and playing games with them. When they were finally tired enough I let them lay in some long grass and promised I would keep watch over them for the night so they would be safe.

As they were lying next to one another I overheard Imari whispering to Karamu, 'I'm sorry I haven't been here for you as much recently Karamu,' he said. 'I've spent so much time with Zarifa I've ignored you. I have had to help her after Talib saved me, but I shouldn't have forgotten our bond.' He kissed her on the cheek. 'When I saw that lioness chasing you, I was so scared. Even more scared than seeing what happened to Talib. The thought of losing you made me feel sick. I ran after you before I thought of anything else. I love you Karamu. And I am so proud to be your brother.'

Karamu shuffled closer to him and they snuggled together as they fell asleep.

'Mbali, this is Abiade,' said my father as he and Jelani returned from their morning meeting with the elders. 'He is very shy but is excited to meet you.'

'Hello Abiade,' she said, kneeling down next to him. 'My name is Mbali, I am Jelani's wife. And this is my daughter Ayana.'

'He...he...hello,' he said quietly.

'And this is Berko, Ayana's husband and his family. His mother Amara, his brother Imari and Karamu his sister. You have already met his father Imamu too.'

'You...you are Berko? I ha...ha...have heard about you.'

'Welcome to our family,' I said, my face getting warmer.

'Wa...wow. Th...thank you for ha...having me.

'Would you like to come and sit down with us for a while Abiade? Before we start walking again?' asked Mbali.

'I would like that ve..very much. Th..thank you.

'Can he come and play with us Mbali?' asked Karamu.

'Maybe later if he feels up to it Karamu. And if he wants to of course?'

'I wou...would love to. Thank you.'

Karamu got really excited and went back over to Imari. 'He's lovely isn't he?' She said, and Imari smiled at her.

10
Coming Full Circle

We were tantalisingly close to the sacred lands of the south and our excitement grew whenever we spotted a familiar sign of the area. The grasses were getting sweeter by the day and the rains were falling frequently, so the walk had been comfortable the past few weeks. And as our excitement grew, the trek became easier to bear, in our minds at least. However, Ayana and the other pregnant females were finding the journey testing now they were all so heavy with calf, and needed the sustenance of the grasslands to keep them going.

I found myself worrying about Ayana a lot, and I offered to help whenever I could, like if we crossed small rivers or the terrain got difficult to negotiate, but she said she could manage and got quite annoyed at me for pestering her. I was getting really protective as we got nearer the sacred lands too. Every time she stopped to rest I kept guard, standing over her to ensure she was safe. I know she is strong and more than capable of looking after herself, but when I think of her precious cargo, I can't help but get worried.

I could tell when I had tested Ayana's patience, so I tried to spend more time with my siblings and Abiade. Despite the circumstances, his arrival into our family came at a good time, both for him and for Karamu. He was really positive for Karamu; his shyness meant she had to be more forthright, and this led her to grow in confidence. Imari encouraged their relationship, telling Karamu to spend time with Abiade and help him to grow more confident too. And with her confidence came real maturity, she's truly blossomed these past few months and is now similar to Imari in her behaviour.

I was happy to see my siblings' relationship was stronger than ever too. After Imari's talk, Karamu was much more relaxed. She was happy to let him go and spend time with Zarifa as well as their other friends from our troop because it gave her a chance to spend time with Abiade. And then she really cherished the time she spent with Imari when he returned.

I had more lessons with father on our journey south. He is still keen to teach me everything there is to know about the land and how to lead the herd to safety. I have become very adept now at reading the signs and predicting the storms. It is one thing to listen for the thunder, but another to know which storm has actually produced rain. Father taught me how to detect the rain on the air; the scent, the feel of the breeze and even how to see rain falling in the distance. He told me one of the elder's old proverbs, 'not everyone who chases the loudest storm catches the rain,' which basically means that not every storm brings with it the rains we all rely on for our survival. So chasing the rain across this vast land, without first reading all the signs the storm is truly showing you, could lead you to a dry desolate pasture which would be costly for the entire herd. So I have to learn how to correctly read the signs I have been shown, but also to trust my true instincts.

Father has also been teaching me how to look within myself these past few months; it is this skill that makes for the truest of leaders. He tells me the teachings are helpful to learn, but the basics are essential. We all have the knowledge of these plains within us, and the memories of our ancestors are passed down through our generations. So if we truly learn to look inside ourselves, then we can see the signs the plains are showing us. I was splitting my time with father between lessons and meditation and I think I am starting to realise how much this earth has to show us.

Since we met with the eland further north, and the rhinos and giraffe at the Nusu Woodlands, the herd were far more relaxed. I think it's because we felt complete again. It's strange how things can feel so different when there are only tiny changes, but you only really notice when it returns to normal. Kwame rejoined the leaders and his fresh perspective helps them all to make clearer decisions. The female eland and giraffe were a massive support to the pregnant wildebeest and the zebra. And the youngsters were having more fun too, chasing each other around and losing themselves in their games whenever we stopped for the day. It was great to see the herd brought together as one large family again.

The herd stopped at a particularly sweet pasture. The long grasses the zebra love had dried quickly, so they were still a vibrant green and packed full of nutrients. As they were clearing this hay, they exposed the best grass we had tasted in a long time. We were all working our way across the plain in large lines so we could all benefit from the succulent fodder. The gazelle were saying how the small blades of fresh growth were packed so full of moisture that it was almost like they were drinking alongside their meal. The leaders told us we should stay in the area for the next few days and really make the most of the nutrient rich grass it has to offer. It would be good for the females to fill up on this so it provides them with the strength they need for birthing. It will also benefit the unborn calves and ensure they are strong and healthy when their time to join us finally arrives.

My father tore me away from Ayana for a while and asked if I'd join him and some of the leaders. We met Jelani, Kwame, Afia, Idriis and Hekima who were sat on a large flat rock overlooking the herd.

'Beautiful isn't it?' Idriis was saying to the others as I arrived. 'The herd and the land in perfect harmony. Ah Berko, glad you could join us.'

'Hey, it's good to see you Berko,' said Kwame, 'congratulations again on your joining with Ayana. Sorry if I embarrassed you the other day.'

'Hi Kwame, thanks. It's ok, I wasn't embarrassed.'

'Oh, I'll have to try harder next time then,' he laughed. 'Your father was telling me about your lessons and how much you have progressed. I always knew you had it in you to lead this herd.'

'Yes, I'm really enjoying my lessons. I still have so much more to learn when I look at all of you though.'

'You are a natural my boy,' said Idriis, 'you have always had the skills. You just needed the confidence to see it within yourself. I have watched you since the beginning Berko. Since you took your first steps on the sacred lands to the south. I have always known you were destined for greatness, and that you would one day prove yourself. I told your father at the start of this year's circle that there is something very special about you. I saw your spirit when you were born. Brighter than the Serengeti sun. Your first ever action in life just proved what I already knew.'

'My first action? What do you mean?'

Jelani stood up and answered my question. 'You helped my daughter Berko. You saved Ayana like you have so many times since.'

'As you know, you were both born on the same day,' continued Idriis. 'But when Ayana entered into this world, her soul was unable to find her.' I sat down on the rock with the others; my legs went weak at hearing this. 'Mbali had a difficult birth. Ayana should have arrived around the same time as you; it's why your mothers were birthing partners. You came into the world, healthy and strong. Your mother cleaned you quickly and you were soon up and feeding. But as your coat was still drying in the morning sun, Ayana had still not arrived. The sun passed right overhead, and all the other new mothers gave birth and took their calves to meet family members. But Mbali just got weaker, and Ayana seemed like she would never arrive. It is not the common practice, in fact it goes against our traditions entirely, but we allowed Jelani to enter the birthing area before the birth so he could be with Mbali,' he looked over to Jelani who looked down solemnly. 'Ayana finally appeared when the sun was almost down, but the labour was unsuccessful, and Mbali was just too exhausted. We all tried to comfort her and Jelani, but it was a difficult time for everyone.'

Jelani came over and touched his forehead to mine and then sat beside me. 'Your mother and father couldn't get you to leave the birthing grounds. As hard as they tried, you seemed to refuse. You were strong; you were up and walking really quickly, but you wouldn't allow your parents to take you out to the pasture. You just dug your tiny hoofs deeper into the grass.'

'Your mother and father sat with her parents to try and help them come to terms with their awful loss, but you went straight over to Ayana. I watched as you pressed her chest with your tiny hoof and prodded her frantically to wake her up. You cleaned her coat and never left her side the entire time. And that is when I saw it. I saw a glowing light. It was shining all around you. Your golden spirit Berko. You pressed her chest again as if to wake her from her sleep, and she let out the smallest cough, almost silent, but I heard it. And when I ran over to you both she was starting to move and trying to sit up. Mbali rushed to her and Ayana fed for the first time. It was a true miracle of the savannah.'

'If it wasn't for you Berko, we would never even have Ayana. *You* are her spirit guide,' said Jelani as tears rolled down his cheeks.

I couldn't speak, and when I tried I broke down. 'Wh...why has nobody told me this before?' I finally said through the tears.

'Your parents always wanted to tell you. As did Jelani and Mbali. But I had to ask them not to Berko,' said Idriis sitting down with me and Jelani. 'As I said, I saw your spirit, the purest spirit there is. It showed itself at that moment. And it brought Ayana back from the stars,' he touched his cheek to mine. 'The brightest spirit had chosen you Berko. But I had to see how you proved yourself into adulthood. I knew you were special.'

'If we had told you about that day, or that you had a bright future, you could easily have let that get the better of you,' said father with tears in his eyes as he and the others sat with us. 'We had to let you grow naturally and forge your own path in life. You had to find your place in the herd and let your destiny find you. And I am so proud of what you have shown us, and who you have become. I am truly proud that you are my son.'

'But I haven't proved myself. I've never tried to be the wildebeest you all talk about.'

'And that is why you are so perfect Berko,' said Idriis. 'You have never felt the need to prove yourself to the others. Even though you are the son of Imamu, you have never tried to stand out, and yet you have shown loyalty, bravery and great leadership,' he stood up and looked over the herd before turning back to look at me. 'When we lost dear Talib, you stepped up and helped the leaders get the youngsters from the water. When Ayana was almost attacked by the river, you stepped in without a second thought and saved her life. And only recently you chased a lioness and saved your brother and sister.'

'It was Imari who acted with bravery,' I said, almost cutting Idriis off. 'He chased that lioness before I could even react.'

He came over to me and I stood up. He touched his forehead to mine as a sign of true respect. 'And even now you put others success above your own,' he touched my cheek. 'When Hatari challenged you to the rut, you accepted, just to prove his disloyalty and to protect the herd from his actions, even though you knew you could get hurt in the process. You are one of the strongest in your age group and you have the highest level of respect from everyone, yet you don't put yourself above others. You are humble Berko; this is such a special quality. You think of everyone else

CHASING THE RAIN

before yourself. And you are modest. When someone recognises you have done well, you don't even realise you have done anything to deserve that recognition. You have become a wonderful young wildebeest Berko.'

The others got to their feet and walked over to us. They all touched their foreheads to mine and stood around me. Then my father did the same and stood next to Idriis.

'When we lost Talib everyone thought it would be impossible to replace him. They felt there would never be another who could lead this herd the way he did. But I always knew. I always knew the brightest spirit would prove their place within this herd. You asked why I wanted your help at the Grumeti. It is because you have shown me more good qualities in your three and a half years than many show throughout their entire lives,' he looked around the group and they all nodded to him and smiled proudly. Then he turned back to look at me. 'There is a reason I have asked you to join me here today Berko. We would like to ask if you would step into dear Talib's place. To walk and to work at our sides,' he dipped his head to me, the sign of respect. 'Would you honour us, and the memory of Talib, by accepting a place as a leader of this herd?'

I stood silent. I was in complete shock at everything he'd said, and I wasn't even sure if this was real anymore. They were all looking at me and still smiling proudly, waiting for my response. I didn't know what to say or do, or what the formality should even be in this situation. I felt my throat closing with nerves and I couldn't speak, so I bowed to them all as they did to me. 'I would be honoured to join you,' I said finally, looking up from my lowered position, but my voice was broken and the words came out as a squeak. I felt my face getting warmer as my embarrassment grew. And then they all came closer and cheered. They all came over one by one and touched my cheeks before congratulating me.

Afia was the last to kiss me and as she did, she whispered 'I am proud of you Berko. Now you can relax and be yourself. Oh, and give Kwame as good as he gives you.' She smiled and winked as she moved back.

'Right, we better get back to our families before they wonder where we are,' said Kwame. 'After you Berko,' he said, and then he bowed at me sarcastically and laughed, nudging me playfully as I walked past.

Our stay in these pastures had drawn to an end. Storms to the south had been rumbling intensely for the past day and night, and the breeze brought with it the smell of hope. There were promising signs of heavy rains ahead of us, so the grasses on our route would be even more succulent than these. We were only a couple of days from the sacred lands and if the storms were as good as they appeared, then we would be in for a very pleasant stay.

I kept the story of Ayana's birth to myself, even though the leaders said I could tell her. I was shocked to hear it, and to learn that my connection to her runs so deeply. I was unable to think of much else the past few days, so I didn't want to burden Ayana when she already had so much on her mind. I was starting to understand why Idriis kept it from me, and I know our parents would have followed the elder's advice. But I kept going over it and couldn't decide if I had a right to know.

Walking south through the open plains, we could sense the promise of the sacred lands coming to fruition. The grasses were even sweeter and the earth seemed to be guiding us home on a path of riches. The openness of the land allowed the breeze to flow all around us and in between the falling rain the air was far less humid. The seekers told us the sacred lands were only a day away, but there was less urgency in the herd now. The females were finding the last stages difficult, and their pace had slowed to a crawl. The males in the herd and the females without calf were helping them all to walk when they could and offering them shelter and protection when they needed to rest. The herd was working as one now we were almost home, and our reward would be the sacred lands we all long for.

There was a message from the leaders that we would stop and rest for the remainder of the day so we could make the final approach at first light. When we set foot in the southern lands, many of the animals will spread out to make the most of the area, so it was decided that tonight we would have a celebration before we got there.

The mention of a celebration had lifted the mood of the herd, and as the time approached, everyone started to gather before the message of its commencement was even passed around. The vast sea of animals stood around the plain, watching as the leaders prepared for the ritual. It would give us all the chance to thank the stars and the guiding spirits for leading us all to the lands we call our home.

Every elder of the herd huddled together in the middle of the plain as they waited for the last members of the herd to join the crowd. After one last glance over their shoulders, they stomped their hoofs once in unison, sending a deep thud that could be felt in all our chests. As one they all turned to face out from the centre and looked over the entire herd. They stomped again and let out a loud '*Roho*' from deep within their throats.

The leaders from all of the droves formed a circle and began to walk in synchronised hoofsteps around the elders. And as they trotted, they shook the dust from within their coats which fell in soft clouds towards their hoofs.

Picking up the pace, the leaders cantered around the elders and the dust filled the air inside the circle.

Idriis broke away from the group and stepped into the dust to begin the ceremony. 'Thank you spirits for your guidance and your teachings,' he called towards the skies in his loud, booming voice. 'You have led us once again to the safety of the sacred lands. Just as you have for millennia. You have given us all the strength to make this journey around your precious savannah.'

'*Roho*,' chanted the elders and they stomped again.

'You showed me a sign,' continued Idriis. 'One I have been waiting so long to see. And I would like to give thanks for what you have offered.'

'*Roho*,' the elders stomped.

All the leaders began to slow and Idriis looked upon the herd. 'I call forward Berko, the son of Imamu, to the sacred circle.'

'*Roho*' the elders stomped twice.

My stomach dropped at hearing my name. Ayana nudged me and I reluctantly made my way through the crowd. Father and Jelani split apart to form a gap, and I stepped through it quickly so I wouldn't trip them as they trotted.

'Spirits, we make you our offering,' shouted Idriis.

'*Roho*' the elders stomped again.

My heart stopped with fear. What were they about to do to me?

'For years I have asked that you show me our destiny,' continued Idriis in a serious and powerful voice. 'And you showed me the brightest spirit among this herd.'

'*Roho*' stomp, stomp.

'The brightest this herd has ever known.'

'*Roho*' stomp, stomp.

'This spirit shows strength and loyalty and honour.'

'*Roho*' stomp, stomp.

'That only the truest leader could possess.'

Stomp... Stomp... Stomp...

'Spirits! We offer you our deepest gratitude and our unending devotion.'

Stomp... Stomp... Stomp...

'And we accept your gift.'

Stomp... Stomp... Stomp...

'We accept the golden spirit.'

Stomp... Stomp... Stomp...

'And we all acknowledge Berko as this herd's newest leader.'

'*Rohooooooo*'

Silence fell over the savannah.

The dust inside the circle lifted all at once and the air cleared.

Then the entire herd erupted into cheers. Everyone started chanting my name in unison. Even my old friends were cheering joyously.

And as I slowly spun and looked all around me, the entire herd bowed down as one.

I was overwhelmed. I couldn't believe they'd all accepted me into all of their hearts.

After the celebrations, members of the herd kept coming over and congratulating me. Wildebeest were saying they were so proud of me. Zebra were telling me the spirits had chosen wisely. Gazelle, eland and elephants were touching their cheeks to mine. I was stunned. I've never found it easy to accept the praise of others, and now I am getting it from everyone in the herd.

My siblings finally had a chance to speak to me, and Karamu was staring at me in admiration. She kept making silly comments about me being the king of the herd, so I had to keep reassuring her that I was only joining the other leaders and working alongside our father. Imari pressed his cheek to mine and whispered in my ear, 'I knew you would do it. I saw this coming for you Berko.' When I asked what he meant he just said 'you know? Because you are the greatest wildebeest I know,' and he smiled before pressing his cheek to mine again.

When the commotion had finally died down and the herd had gone off into their little groups again to talk, I took Ayana aside and said I wanted to talk privately. 'That sounds worrying Berko,' she said.

We sat away from the herd and I told her the full story of her birth. I also let her know that Idriis had told everyone they couldn't mention it. She sat there in silence for a while and I waited for some sort of a reaction from her. Then, when I could hardly bear it any more she finally spoke.

'That explains everything,' she said, and she kissed me. 'It explains why you've always been the only wildebeest I could talk to so freely. Why you stood up for me in the nursery group. It explains why every time I'm in any kind of danger you are there to protect me. You *are* my spirit guide. I have always wanted to see mine. Whenever others talk about theirs, I'd get jealous, annoyed even, because I feared I was on this earth alone. But now it's so clear, I have been able to see my spirit all along. I always had you. You were always there for me Berko. You were right in front of me my entire life.' She pressed her cheek to mine and then kissed me again.

'But the leaders kept this from us. Aren't you upset?'

'Idriis has this herd's best interest at heart. That's why we all trust his decisions. He would have done this for a reason,' she said. 'Our fate is already written in the stars Berko. But we have to learn it for ourselves. If we'd been given this knowledge from a young age then we may have forced ourselves to be together. We would never have learnt so much about each other. I may never have fallen for the true Berko. And you would never have fallen for me,' she kissed my cheek. 'It is your personality that I love Berko. It is the way you make me feel and the way you are always there for me no matter what. That has all happened naturally and it's made our relationship as strong as it is. You can't force that between two beings.'

'I guess in some way, I always knew. I knew I loved you as soon as I saw you. And I knew I never wanted to be apart from you.'

'And I love you Berko.' She pressed her body against mine and we stared into the stars and listened to the laughter and joy across the herd.

Now we are in the sacred lands, the herd have spread out to make the most of the pastures and the open plains. We spend so many months travelling and walking so closely to each other, it is good to be able to breathe at last. Our offspring will start to arrive after around thirty days of being here, but the females are now finding it very difficult. When they need to eat, we feed in large groups surrounding them all so they don't have to be as vigilant; this gives them more opportunity to eat in the short time they can stand up. Much of their time however is spent laying or sitting in the grass, resting their legs and reserving their energy for the birthing process. Once the time arrives, they will all come together and stay in large nursing groups before entering the sacred birthing area. There they can watch over each other as they give birth and help each other through the process of labour.

We have long felt safe in this area; our ancestors found there was a good supply of food and water, and plenty of open space so the herd can watch for danger. This is why we feel able to remain here and await the arrival of our offspring, as well as stay and allow our new arrivals to get used to their legs and learn the skills they will need for the start of their lives. But as we have used this area for millennia, so too have our enemies. They soon learned it was an area the wildebeest and the zebra favoured, so they quickly developed plans to head for the area around the same time as us. They set up camps on the outskirts and they watch for weak or lame animals among us.

Over the millennia, we have come to an unspoken agreement with the enemy. If the herd is faced with a loss of one of our own, either through the stress of birth or one of the young is born without life, then the enemy can take the body. We have long believed when we die, our soul escapes the vessel of our form very quickly and awaits our herd to perform the ritual that carries the soul up to the stars to sit among the other spirits. And we believe by offering the vessel to the enemy, they can be fed and the spirits will protect the living. Our enemies tend to follow this rule for much of the time; however there are always those among the enemy, like Hatari within our herd, who will go against the rules of the savannah and the teachings of our ancestors. There are always those who will try to take what is not theirs and attempt to snatch a young or a weak member of the herd before it is time. So we always stay vigilant for the sake of the females.

The closer we get to the arrival of our young, I am becoming more anxious. I've barely prepared myself for fatherhood and the idea that I will soon have someone depending on me is terrifying. Ayana went to spend time with Mbali and my mother to talk about the birthing process, so I went and found my father. Before I could say anything, he looked at me and smiled. 'First time nerves Berko? We all had that. Come, sit with me.'

'How do you know if you are ready to be a father?'

'You can never be truly ready my son, it doesn't matter how much you prepare yourself. I was as nervous as you are. I thought I would never be able to look after a calf. I looked at many of my friends, those who had chosen the tradition of the harem. I wondered if I had made the right choice in joining with your mother in marriage because many of my friends had no responsibilities. I even thought about devoting more time to my leadership to let your mother raise you alone, I worried that my fears would be more of a hindrance to your mother and she would be better off if I stayed away. But when you entered the world, all of those fears and thoughts just vanished. As soon as I saw your tiny face looking up at me I knew my entire world was right there in front of me. Your mother had carried you across the expanse of this earth and the spirits had delivered you to me in the sacred lands. When I saw the love in your eyes and how happy you made your mother, I knew that you were precious. And I knew I could be a father.'

'But I'm scared I won't know what to do.'

'Berko, did you know what to do when the crocodile leapt from the lake at Ayana?'

'No... I just acted.'

'When life throws something at you, you will know how to deal with it in your own way. I didn't know how to be a father and now I have three incredible children. I didn't know what to do or how to act, but I cared for you, nurtured you and taught you what I know.'

'And you are a great father.'

'Thank you Berko,' he squeezed me lovingly. 'And you will be too my son. Look within you, the knowledge is there, just like the knowledge of this land. You just need to find it.'

The herd had been feeding around the outskirts of the chosen birthing area for the last few weeks and the patch that was left was thick with brush. This would allow the females to bed down when the time comes and hide while their offspring arrive. The cover provided by the grasses offers both a safe haven from our enemies, and privacy from the males. The land was blessed by all of the elders before it was left untouched, so it would be cleansed in preparation for the new arrivals.

Ayana kept watching the area closely, 'I wish you could be there when our calf arrives Berko,' she said. Our traditions dictate that the females must birth with other females. The only males that may enter during the birthing process are the elders. It's said the other males are not permitted so the area is kept clear for the spirits to find the young, but I know it is really to just keep us out of the way as we tend to get more worried than the females.

'As soon as you give birth I will be at your side. I wish I could be there throughout too,' I kissed her cheek tenderly. But in truth I feel I would just add to her stress if I was with her. 'Do you want to take a walk around the nursing area? To find the perfect spot for you. That way I'll know where you'll be and can get to you quickly.'

'I would like that,' she said and kissed my cheek in return.

The area was vast to allow many females to bed down at one time, so we had to take lots of breaks for Ayana to rest. It took us most of the afternoon to finally walk around the outskirts, but we finally found a nice area that she liked. It would provide her with more shelter as the grasses were already longer than the rest and it was marked by an old termite mound that I could easily recognise if she was rushed to the area before I was told. The activity was mainly to take her mind off it all and she seemed much happier. But thinking so much about the process brought home the reality of the arrival of my child, and it made me more scared than I had felt since Ayana told me she was pregnant.

I wanted to spend some time with my siblings now we have made it to the south. They have been a little neglected with all the preparations for the females. They are a little way off this stage in their lives, so it is of no real interest to them. Karamu is a bit more excited than Imari as she's looking forward to seeing the new baby when it comes. But most of the preparations are for the adults to attend, so the youngsters end up hanging around with some of the elders until they become quite bored of their stories.

I asked if Abiade wanted to join us, and we all went to play in the grasslands. We played a few games of Ampe and then had a game of chase. When they were tired out we all sat and relaxed in the long grass. It was nice to speak with Abiade now that he has grown in confidence; he is really finding himself with Mbali and the family, and Ayana has started to see him as her little brother. But I think it is Karamu that has brought him the most happiness. He told me how Karamu made him feel accepted and helped him to see that family doesn't have to be through blood. He was extremely sad when his mother passed away, but he thinks she guided Mbali to him. It was fate that brought them together and love that makes their bond stronger. Karamu wanted to play again so she and Abiade went and played Ampe some more and left me and Imari sat in the grass.

'Do you like him?' asked Imari.

'Abiade? Of course I do.'

'Me too. He's good for Karamu. And he'll make her happy in the future.'

'Yes they do seem to be getting on well.'

Imari sat up and turned to me. 'He has a good spirit Berko. He is going to be good for this herd.'

I sat up too. 'What do you mean Imari?'

'I haven't said anything to father. Or anyone else. Because I'm still trying to work out what's happening,' he said looking serious. 'But I have seen Abiade before.'

'You know him?'

'No. I saw him in one of my dreams,' he said looking almost through me. 'He came into our family and he married Karamu. He became the next leader and stood by your side.'

'When did you have this dream Imari? Was it recent?'

'No, it was before we even met with the eland again. Long before those lionesses attacked.' I touched my cheek to his. 'But like I said, I think he will be a leader. Like you Berko.'

'I probably shouldn't say this Imari,' I paused. 'But the leaders have their eye on you. They see something great. I think it might be you by my side.'

'I know. I saw that too. But I won't be there as a leader like you Berko. I'm needed like Idriis and Talib.

I'm needed to read the spirits of others. But Abiade is going to be important. For the herd and for you.'

I looked straight at Imari; I couldn't tell now if he was joking like he often does. But he seemed deadly serious. 'What else have you seen Imari?'

'Lots of things. But many of them don't seem like they could be real,' he said as he looked back at me, right into my eyes this time. 'Shirika told me that Talib saw something in me. And that I was like him. I have always had vivid dreams, like all those I've told you about. And sometimes when I'm not even asleep. In my last dream about Talib, he was stood in the ceremonial circle again. He bowed to you and Ayana as Idriis announced your joining together. Then he told me to trust in myself, seeing is believing. I kept hearing it in my head for ages after that dream, and then I thought about all the other things I'd seen before, like the attack on Thairu and poor Duni by the river. Like you, I thought they were just my memories getting jumbled up or something, but recently I've been seeing more of the things from my dreams come true. Like Ayana being pregnant, I tried to look shocked, but I knew she was going to tell us. I saw you becoming a leader, and your ceremony. And then there was Abiade, I knew he would join us.'

I sat in silence for a while, unable to speak to him. I watched Karamu laughing as she chased Ayana's new brother around. 'So why is Abiade so important?' I said finally.

'I don't know yet. I know his mother was from a good blood line. I think her grandfather was an elder. But I've haven't been able to see any clarity in her.' He looked away for a second and then back at me. 'You believe me don't you Berko?'

CHASING THE RAIN

I breathed deeply and nodded. 'I do Imari. I have no reason to doubt you.'

'I am glad Karamu will be happy. I couldn't bear it if she wasn't. It's her happiness that feeds my soul Berko,' he said looking over at the two of them playing. 'She's my spirit guide. I thought she needed me. That's why I've always been there for her. But I know now that it's the other way around. It's me who needs Karamu. And now she has found true love, her spirit is growing stronger each day.'

'You think she loves Abiade?'

'I know she does. She doesn't know it yet, but she loves him,' he looked back at me with that serious expression. 'You can't tell her what I've said Berko, please. She can't know. You cannot make fate work in your favour. She's got to learn her feelings for herself. Promise me you won't say anything Berko.'

'You have my word Imari,' I touched my forehead to his. 'You have matured so much, in such a short time. And I'm impressed at how you've dealt with such a gift on your own. If you want to tell father, I can be there with you. He could talk to Idriis for you. Give you some guidance.'

'Thanks Berko, but I think I will give it some time. I may be maturing, but I'm not ready to sit through lessons all day just yet. And I need to learn how to read my dreams better. Once I know for sure if it is even true, I'll seek father's guidance.'

I gave him a hug and we sat watching Karamu laughing with Abiade. And as they played, the more I believed what Imari had just told me.

The first of the females went into labour today and there is real excitement among the herd. There's a strong energy in the air like that of the start of one of our ceremonies. The offspring could arrive anytime from now, and the last of the young could take around thirty days to come, so the excitement probably won't last too long.

The female who gave birth first had the help from other members of her harem. When she came out of the birthing grounds the elders all blessed her and her calf; being the first of the season is thought to be a lucky sign for the mother. She took her newborn out into the pasture to be alone with her and the male checked her over to make sure she was healthy before he went back to enjoy the sunshine with all the other males. Although this is the most common tradition our troop follow, I find it difficult to see a young mother alone at such a difficult time. And I know she will have the support of the other females soon, but it seems like the male of the harem has little to no interest in his own child. Choosing to be with Ayana for the rest of my life may not be the usual tradition, but in my heart I know our child will benefit from having us both there throughout its childhood, like we both had our parents through ours.

We have started to see some of our enemies around the grasslands these past few days. We spend our entire lives trying desperately to avoid them at all costs, but during this time it is completely different. Because we have had the agreement for so long, they know they need to be patient. I even spoke to a lioness who was feeding her new cubs today. She told me how she was happy to have three healthy babies and she even wished me luck for Ayana. New life seems to bring out the good in everyone.

'Berko! It is time,' called mother. 'Ayana has entered labour; we are taking her to the birthing grounds now.'

I ran over to Ayana and kissed her, 'I will be right here Ayana. Call for me when you need to.' Mbali and mother led her in through the tall grass and I sat down in the shadow of the termite mound, dragging my hoof through the grass in nervous scrapes. My stomach was churning and I was nauseous even though I hadn't eaten anything all morning, I could barely imagine how Ayana must be feeling.

My family came to sit with me, and Jelani and Abiade joined us too. 'Do you think she will be ok?' I asked my father.

Imari placed his hoof on mine and nodded at me while giving me a reassuring smile. 'I think she will be just fine Berko,' he said and he winked.

The shadow of the termite mound swept around to cover each of us at some point while we waited, and although I felt comforted by Imari's words, I still couldn't fully relax. Father was trying to keep Jelani's mind off it by talking about the beautiful weather, but he saw straight through it. Karamu called to mother to see how things were going and mother invited her in as she was the only one among us allowed to set foot inside the circle during the birth.

I stood up and started to pace back and forth, 'it's taking too long,' I said frantically.

Then, just as father was going to speak, Karamu's head popped out of the thick long grass with a huge, beaming smile on her face. 'Berko, come quickly.'

I entered through the thick grass, following Karamu closely. As we came to the end of the tall grasses, I could see my mother on the left and Mbali on the right. And sat in a flattened patch was Ayana. Laying in the curve of her body was the smallest wildebeest I have ever seen.

'Berko, say hello to your new son.' He looked up at me shivering, his fur still wet, his ears hanging limply each side of his tiny head, and his huge eyes looking straight into my soul.

'He is perfect,' I said through tears of pure joy.

Karamu went back out the way she came and brought the others back one by one. They told me afterwards they had all visited, but I hadn't noticed, I just stood admiring the two most amazing beings in my life.

'Have you thought of a name Berko?' asked Ayana.

'Me?' I paused. 'I can only think of one that would suit him Ayana. What about Azizi?'

'Precious? I like that very much,' she looked down at him. 'Azizi, our precious son.'

I stayed with Ayana and Azizi among the tall grasses until our son had fed and learned to stand on his tiny hoofs. We made our way out carefully as Azizi was still very wobbly on his feet, and as we exited the tall grass the lioness looked over at me and smiled, 'he is beautiful,' she said. 'You must be so proud.' Her three cubs waved to my son with excitement and Ayana looked at me a little perplexed.

We headed over to the pasture to let Azizi get used to his legs and Ayana had a bite to eat to get her strength back. Our son stumbled around and fell down several times, but he soon got back to his hoofs and tried again; quickly mastering the difficult task. As I looked around the plain, already blossoming with so much new life, Azizi was by far the smallest in his age group. He even struggled to reach his mother, so Ayana needed to lower herself slightly for him to feed. But as I watched the others still trying to stand for more than a few seconds, I could already tell he was going to do well on this savannah.

Shirika and Zarifa came to see our son and they were in awe. Karamu came charging over and asked if she could take him to sit with the youngsters for a while. We were a bit worried at first but we decided to let them go. We spoke to Shirika, and our mothers came and joined us to talk too. And as we talked, I kept looking over to make sure he was ok. It was true what my father said; you don't know how to be a father, but fatherhood certainly knows how to find you.

A little later, Ayana and I took Azizi away from the herd to sit on our own for the first time all day. As I stared at them both and watched Azizi snuggle into Ayana, I realised I had everything. Azizi fell asleep and Ayana turned to me and whispered 'do you think he will be ok Berko?' He is so tiny and fragile.'

'He is perfect my love. With our love and our nurturing he will grow stronger every day. And with such a loving family, he will never want for anything.'

Over the next few days Azizi was finding it much easier to feed and Ayana didn't need to help him anymore. I was spending all of my time with them both and Azizi was doing well. He started to speak and can say many words already. And he is getting to know all of our families well. He loves his aunty and uncles, and although we need to allow them to play with him, I found myself worrying. He is still very small, smaller than the other newborns, but he is doing better than most of them. Although he has only learnt to walk recently he is already able to keep up with my siblings and is enjoying the odd game of chase with them. Karamu has taken a supportive role, helping Ayana with his care when she needs it. She is showing real maturity and impresses me more each day.

I took Imari and Karamu to one side while Ayana fed Azizi. 'I have been speaking with Ayana,' I said to them both. 'We'd like to ask you both if you would like to be Azizi's protectors. When we have his naming ceremony, you would both get to be involved. Would you honour us in accepting these roles?' They both looked really happy.

'I'd love to,' screamed Karamu excitedly. 'So... what is a protector?' she asked.

'If anything should happen to me or Ayana, you will step in as Azizi's guardian. You will protect him and look after him until he is old enough to look after himself. We both think you have shown such maturity these past months, and we'd be honoured to bestow this responsibility on you both.'

'Then I'd love to,' she said again.

Imari smiled proudly, 'I would love that too. I didn't even see that coming,' he said excitedly.

The Remaining females have all given birth now and the plain is bursting with new life. The majority of our enemies stuck to the agreement, but there were some attacks by those who couldn't fight against their instincts. It is inevitable when we are all packed into one area for such a long time that our enemies will take any opportunity they get to feed; after all we are surrounded by endless luscious grass and are fattening up well for the new journey north.

Azizi is doing well in the nursery group and has already made many friends. He has grown quickly and has even grown larger than some of the others his own age. Ayana has been making new friends in the nursery group too and has been helping the newest mothers cope with their offspring. She has truly taken to motherhood and seems to be a natural.

Whilst Ayana is spending time with the other new mothers, I've taken the opportunity to spend some time with the leaders to make plans for the new journey. They've all helped me settle in and I've even been able to give my input this time. I am still struggling to see myself as equal due to my inexperience, but they have all said they like my fresh perspective on the plans. During the meetings we discuss every possible outcome of the journey. And although the herd won't be moving out again until the grasses get too dry for us to feed, father tells me it is always best to be prepared. Idriis said he looks forward to working with me on the next circle and thinks I will be fine despite my nerves and my age, and I'm feeling less anxious at every meeting. Father has been talking non-stop about Azizi, more than I have in fact, but it's good to see him beaming with such pride.

I found out recently that Imari has been getting close to one of Karamu's friends Mila. He's been keeping it from his sister in case she got upset, but when Mila told her, she was thrilled.

Karamu has been spending more time with Abiade and he is really confident now. He has been looking out for Karamu far more lately too. She is still helping with Azizi in her spare time and has been taking the role of protector to her heart. She is excited about the naming ceremony in a few days and has been talking about it all the time. I must admit, I too have become quite excited about it, because it will make my fatherhood seem that little bit more real.

Today I finally had a chance to spend time with my own family. Ayana, Azizi and I went and sat among the long, dry grasses to have a talk alone. Azizi was playing with the hay and we were captivated by the wonder in his eyes as crickets leapt out from beneath their cover. Ayana looked at him lovingly and placed her head tenderly on my shoulder. 'Do you think Azizi will be able to cope with the trek? It is only a month away, she said.'

'I think he will be fine Ayana. He is strong. And much faster than many of the other wildebeest already. He will do well on this journey, I'm sure.'

'You will be spending lots of your time with the leaders, and I will be watching Azizi,' she said as she sat up to look at me. 'Do you think we will be ok Berko?'

'Of course,' I said softly, looking right into her eyes. 'I love you Ayana. I will lead this herd as best I can, but my main priority will always be the two of you. I would never let the leaders make decisions that would put you both at risk,' I kissed her cheek. 'And I will be by your side at every opportunity, I promise. Look at both our fathers; they have done well to spread their time between fatherhood and leadership. I will try my best to be as good as them.' I watched Azizi hitting the grass and giggling when the bugs leapt out at him. 'I was worried about being a father Ayana,' I said finally. 'Mainly because I didn't think I would be able to do it. But my father reminded me I was also unsure about the leadership too, yet I did what was needed because it came naturally to me. And I feel the same with Azizi. The second I saw him I knew I was going to be a good father. Not because I thought I knew how to, or because I know better than anyone else on the savannah. But because I know I would die to protect him. If he needs anything, I will provide it. If he hurts himself, I will kiss it better. And if he struggles with the journey, I would carry him to safety. He is our precious little cargo Ayana, and he is now the most important thing on the Serengeti,' I kissed her cheek once more. 'And if I can prove myself to be even half the parent you are becoming Ayana, then I know Azizi will be fine.' Ayana placed her head on my shoulder again, and we both watched our son as he laughed at the cricket now sat upon his nose.

The sun turned to orange as Azizi walked over and curled up between us. And as we watched it disappearing beneath the horizon I realised how lucky I am.

'Come on everyone, we can't leave Idriis waiting,' I said trying to round up both of my families, 'the naming ceremony starts soon.'

We had asked to have it at first light so we could enjoy the rest of the day as a celebration for all of us. The ceremony is a private affair, which must be overseen by one elder and one other leader. But although a few of us in our family are now in that position, none of us can do it because we are related to Azizi. We decided to ask both Kwame and Afia as they are our closest friends who are also of high enough stature to witness Azizi's ceremony.

We invited a number of guests too, including Kwame's wife and daughters, and Afia's husband and daughter. Shirika and Zarifa are even going to make the journey from the north of the territory to be involved. We wanted them all to be present as they all mean so much to us and we would like them to be as big a part of Azizi's life as they are ours.

Everyone finally got together and we all headed to the sacred grasslands where Azizi was born. The grass was very tall now but starting to dry out at the tips. Karamu led the party in through the wilderness and as we came to the clearing, Idriis was there preparing for the ceremony.

'Ah you are here,' he said and bent down to touch cheeks with Azizi. 'You have grown so quickly my child.' He invited us all in and told each of us where to stand. 'We will start the ceremony as soon as the sun appears.'

Imari went out to stand at the entrance so the guests knew where we'd be, and as Shirika and Zarifa came through the long grass, Imari followed and indicated they were the last of the guests to arrive.

Idriis lined the guests up behind the family and asked them to form a complete circle. Then he stretched his head up high and glimpsed the golden light hitting the tops of the tallest grasses. 'The ceremony is about to begin.' We all fell silent as the breeze rustled through the dry blades.

'As we all stand here to celebrate the newest arrival to both of your families, I would like to just thank you from the bottom of my heart for choosing me as your elder for this ceremony. It brings me great pleasure to welcome your son into the world,' he smiled to us both. 'Spirits,' he boomed, making Azizi jump. 'I present to you this new member of our herd. The son of Berko and Ayana. I ask that you watch over him and guide him safely through his life. I ask that you recognise this wildebeest as Azizi, and guide his spirit to find him on this savannah.' He bowed and then touched his forehead to our son's. 'Berko you are a strong father and I know you will be a wonderful role model for him. Ayana your kindness and strength will nurture Azizi to become a loyal and honest young wildebeest. You will both love him and protect him and he will bring you so much joy. The love you both hold in your hearts and the protection you will want to give to your son will grow ever stronger each day, and the stronger it becomes, the more devoted you will become as parents. It will be a bond that can never be broken.'

He looked towards Kwame and Afia. 'Could the two of you please step forward and stand beside this young child. Do you both agree to bear witness to this child's naming?'

'We do,' they said together.

'And do you agree that the name which has been chosen by his loving parents suits this young wildebeest?'

'We do,' they said again. Idriis nodded and they stepped back to their original positions.

'May I have Imari and Karamu to come forward please? Stand beside him as you will through this life,' he nodded to them both as they got into position. 'I ask the spirits to entrust these two as young Azizi's protectors.' He touched his forehead to Imari's and then to Karamu's. 'Do you both accept the responsibility that has been entrusted to you?'

'We do.'

'And do you promise to help young Azizi, and guide him through this life? To show him the way of the herd if his parents cannot?'

'We do.'

Idriis nodded again and my siblings went back to stand with my parents. 'With all of these animals who have come to be a part of this ceremony, it is clear this young wildebeest will always have someone to look out for him at every turn on his journey into adulthood. He will never want for anything. And he will always have everything he needs. So it gives me great pleasure to welcome you, Azizi, to this herd and to this family.'

Everyone walked around us once and then kissed Azizi on the forehead to symbolise their bond, before exiting through the long grass.

We waited for a while and our parents stayed with us so we could all thank Idriis for the ceremony. 'I was thrilled to be a part of it,' he said and he too kissed Azizi on the forehead to show his bond.

As we exited the sacred grasslands, all of the guests touched their cheeks to ours and thanked us for inviting them. We led the way to one of the small lakes where we could carry on the celebrations for the rest of the morning. We all drank to Azizi and all bonded as one big family.

The party was really good, the adults talked and relaxed in the sun and the youngsters all played with their new nephew. There were games of Ampe and Mbube Mbube, they played chase and drank from the lake when they were all too exhausted. It was the first time in a while we were all able to just stop and live in the moment.

All of the guests enjoyed it and Kwame joked that Ayana and I should have more children so we could do this all again. When we were all tired, we sat together and shared stories and sang songs, and we laughed until our stomachs ached.

When the guests started to leave, the children went off to play some more games in the sun. Abiade stayed behind and came over to sit with us all. 'Can I ask something?' he said to Mbali and Jelani.

'Yes, what is it my son?' said Jelani.

'You have looked after me and have showed me more love and affection than I could have ever wished for. Would you both do me the greatest honour in becoming my new parents?' Mbali had to turn away as tears bubbled up in her eyes. 'When Idriis said those things during the ceremony, about Ayana and Berko, I just knew this was the right decision. I have felt so much love and so much protection from you both; I feel like you really are my parents. When I lost my mother, I was heartbroken, but I knew fate would guide me in some way. And then it brought me to you.'

Jelani grabbed him and held him close. 'It is us who would be honoured Abiade. We could never have believed our wishes would be answered in such a way.' The three of them hugged and even Jelani couldn't hold back the tears.

'Well, I guess Kwame will get his party after all,' said father as we all went over to hug them. 'Would you like me to arrange it with Idriis for you both?'

'That would be fantastic,' said Jelani. 'We will have a ceremony as soon as he can see us.'

Abiade's Ceremony was held the following day when the sun was at its highest. The same guests came and the atmosphere was amazing. The tenderness of the ceremony made it clear this was the right decision, and as a touching tribute, Idriis even added in a memorial to Abiade's birth mother. He made her an honorary protector as she had clearly seen him to safety and to a loving new family, which made the whole thing so much more beautiful. The party afterwards was just like the previous day, we had just as much fun and just as many stories to tell. The youngsters had just as much energy and played games until the sun was almost down.

When most of the youngsters were playing Mbube, Imari came over to talk with me. 'You don't want a ceremony too do you?' I joked.

He looked at me a little perplexed and then said 'I dreamt about Abiade again Berko.'

We walked down towards the lake so we could speak away from all of the adults. 'What did you see in your dream Imari?'

He came closer and lowered his voice. 'I saw his mother. I saw her more clearly than before and she spoke directly to me. She told me about today's ceremony and then everything she said came true. She said it is going to be perfect and the tribute to her will make her so happy. She has always protected him but will cherish her new role. She also asked me to thank Mbali and Jelani for their kindness towards her son. But how would I even do that Berko? I would look crazy if I said any of this to them.'

He looked troubled and although he spoke so maturely, I could tell this was all very difficult for him to deal with. I'm not even sure I am mature enough for any of this. 'I promised I would always be here for you Imari, I will help you as best I can,' I said. 'I'll try my best to help you work out what your dreams are telling you, and I will speak to Mbali. I won't tell her the message came from you, but I will let her know I think Abiade's mother would be happy.'

'Thank you,' he said and he touched his cheek to mine. 'Abiade was born to pure spirits Berko,' he continued. 'His mother was Muhima, a direct descendant of Gikuyu and Mumbi.'

'He has sacred blood?'

'Yes, and like I said before, he will be very important for the herd. She said his blood is pure and his spirit is bright. But his importance will only become clear to me at a time of great need for the herd,' he closed his eyes and tried to remember his vision. 'A... decision he makes will protect us.' He looked over at his sister. 'Because his spirit is brightened by Karamu's love, the event will occur shortly after their first rut.'

'What will happen Imari?'

'I don't know. I can't see it yet. I just know that Abiade will protect us all.'

We have been in the sacred lands for almost three months. The grass is starting to dry out and the water supply is dwindling. We all know the time to leave is fast approaching and the feeling of anxiety is once again upon us. We leaders have made our plans and have gone over them again and again. But despite the number of times we have talked about the journey, there is nothing more we can do now other than return to our families and await the storms to show themselves.

Imari has still been wrestling with his gift. Learning to read what he has seen and determine what is real and what are only dreams has been challenging, but I have been impressed by his maturity in dealing with it all. He still asks that I keep this from the other leaders and confides in me whenever he learns of anything new, saying he has the same amount of respect for me as he does for father. I have promised to help him work it out as best I can, and I am comforted in the knowledge that one day he will be leading this herd by my side.

Karamu has asked my advice about Abiade on a number of occasions, and although I give the same answer, she is still uncertain of her own mind, but I know this will change as she gets older. Her feelings grow stronger whenever they meet up, and she wants to be with him all the time. I tell her to 'just follow your heart; don't let your mind take charge where your feelings are concerned because your spirit will guide you in the right direction.' I am very aware of the things Imari has told me, and I know I can't let Karamu know the truth, so I want her to do what makes her the happiest, and if that is getting closer to Abiade at the risk of losing her other friends, then it is the right decision for her.

Both our parents have really taken to having a grandchild. My father and Jelani love taking Azizi to show him the plains. They are living proof that you can be a good leader and great parents too, and they are more of an inspiration to me now than ever before. My mother has spoken of having more children of her own, and Mbali now feels she's over the fear of Ayana's birth, so she is even planning to try again this season. They've said Ayana and I have taken to parenthood so well that it has encouraged them to expand the family unit, and the support it will give to us all will only add to the joy we all get from having new life among us.

Back with my entire family, the wait is taking its toll. Father is pacing as he always does and his temper is a little short, even though he knows he has the herd's full trust. I know I have the same responsibilities now, but I'm able to turn my attentions to Azizi whenever I'm stressed. I can look through him and see the situation far more clearly. The lack of food and the rationing of water might mean we are spending less time feeding, but to Azizi this just means more time to spend with me and his mother. And the receding grasses expose more and more dirt and dust, but he just sees more places to call his playground. His perception of this land gives me far more clarity. And it helps me to see everything from a completely different angle. We are built to survive, no matter what the stars send our way, so we need to see the savannah for what it truly is; our home. These signs that are shown to us are just preparing us to leave. And they give us more hope that the horizon will hold so much promise.

Azizi is staring into the distance with a look of wonder in his eyes as he watches the horizon, and then there's a sound; the magnificent rumble we've all been wishing to hear. Father breathes a sigh of relief and turns back to us all. 'Only a few more days now,' he says and he smiles just slightly.

The sound resonates throughout the herd and brings hope to all our hearts. The animals know the savannah is calling, and we must ready ourselves and our children for the journey to begin all over again. As everyone spreads out to enjoy the last scraps of these pastures, it gives us all time to reflect on the journeys since passed.

When I started this circle I saw it as just another endless trudge across this vast relentless savannah. But for me, this has truly been a journey. I've discovered so much about myself and even more about those around me. I've discovered the true meaning of love and friendship. Experienced the highest level of respect, and seen animals put their entire trust in others in order to survive what lay in our path. But above all I have learned to be myself. And even though I thought I was not worthy of belief or respect from others, I have been accepted by all those around me, and praised for the choices I've made and the actions I've carried out through my own decisions. I thought I was destined to blend in with this herd; my lines to blur like the hoofprints I make, becoming indecipherable from all of the others. But as Idriis told me; the commitment you make to those around you and the kindness you hold within your heart will always guide the spirits towards the brightest one among the haze.

Our journey around the savannah has been like that of my journey through this life. A continual series of lessons and challenges, and I have become stronger and more mature as I've overcome each one. It's taught me to open my heart to all those around me, and my mind to the savannah itself. Father showed me that we are all born with the teachings of our forefathers already instilled within us, and only when we open ourselves to the savannah's call, can we really see what this land has to offer. In only a year I have learnt so much, and learned to love so many. I've walked side by side through the difficult terrain of life, with animals I can truly call my friends and consider as close as family, and I've helped those who've faced the toughest paths of us all.

I opened myself to Ayana and in return she completed my soul and gave me new life in the form of Azizi. When we held his naming ceremony, I was touched by how many animals wanted to come and show their support for us. And I am humbled that the herd all accepted me into their hearts. Our family is large; it consists of adults and children, elders and leaders; it contains wildebeest, zebra, eland and gazelle, elephants, rhinos and giraffe; the list seems endless, much like the love we all have for one another. It is friendship that brings us together and it is love that creates our strongest bond. Karamu was brought to our family by fate, and our bond with her is stronger than the Maras' roaring current. Our love and devotion gave her strength, and she's used this strength to support Abiade through the toughest of times. And although it was tragedy that brought him to us, Abiade is proof that it takes more than blood to tie us all together.

My decision to marry Ayana was not the usual tradition of the herd, but I know it was right for me. And when I look at our son who has so much yet to learn, I know it was right for Azizi too. I didn't feel mature enough to look after myself when we were last walking these pastures. But now I have this precious child to protect and to nurture, to show the way through this life and to lead to safety along with all of our family, I feel far more grown up and much better prepared. I could never have done any of this if it wasn't for my loved ones, and my son will be so much richer for having them all in his life.

My family are grazing together on a patch of the grasslands and Azizi is getting restless. 'I am going to take Azizi for a walk Ayana, I won't be too long,' I say and she just nods and watches as we head towards the rocky outcrop.

I help my son to clamber onto the large, flat rock overlooking the entire herd. 'We can sit here Azizi, the view is best from this spot,' I say to him.

'Ok daddy,' he says as he sits beside me. We watch everyone in the herd as they feed in preparation for the journey. Now the rains have shown us they're coming, there is less need to ration the grasses. We can all eat what we like once again.

'Can you see there in the distance Azizi? That mass of black and white? Those are our good friends the zebra,' he squints trying to focus on them. 'They will soon rejoin us and you will get to meet Shirika and her daughter properly. You met her at your naming ceremony a while back, but you probably don't remember her,' he shook his head as he tried to recall the guests at the party. 'And when you are a little older I will tell you about our amazing friend Talib. He was the bravest zebra the savannah has ever known,' his eyes widened. 'Can you see how the earth is moving all around down there Azizi? Those are all of your family. This herd is large, and we wildebeest make up most of it. But it is all our good friends that make this herd what it truly is. We are formed of individual animals, but we exist as one. You will learn there is nothing stronger in this world than the love that holds this herd together. And now you are a part of that bond.'

I pointed out how vast the land was and how far it stretched to the horizon, 'we will soon be embarking on an incredible journey Azizi. One that will take us far beyond the horizon and to lands you could hardly even imagine. Everything you see is ours, it belongs to all of the animals on the savannah, even our enemies, and you need to respect the land and all those who walk upon it if you are to make it beyond the horizon. I will teach you everything I know, and I will always be here to protect you my son.' We watched as the sky changed colour, and Azizi curled up next to me in the warm golden glow of the falling sun.

The herd was preparing for the evening. The eland started to feed in the cool evening air while the wildebeest and the gazelle lay down to rest their weary hoofs. The sun was casting golden light across the plain and the shadows of the herd stretched out, far across the earth.

Azizi shuffled himself closer as the cold air surrounded us, so I led down to protect him from the breeze. We both looked out to the horizon to watch the setting sun, and I was reminded again of my looming responsibility. As I thought once more about chasing the rain, I felt a little anxious of my future. But when I saw the innocent wonder in Azizi's wide eyes, I was comforted. Because now I truly understand; no matter where you are on your journey, your guiding spirit will find you. And your true destiny will always be revealed within the stars.

THE END

Acknowledgements

I would like to say a huge thank you to my amazing wife Emily. If it wasn't for your patience and your support then I don't think I would have completed this novel. From reading and re-reading my early drafts to helping me pick the final design for my cover, you have been with me all the way. Thank you so much.

I would also like to say a massive thank you to my family, especially my parents Pat and Pete. You both made me who I am and your love and guidance has been a constant throughout my life. The support and encouragement you have always given me has enabled me to pursue anything I have ever put my mind to.

Another special thank you goes out to my big brother Ben. Some people are lucky to have a best friend and others are lucky to have an amazing sibling, but I have always considered myself to be truly gifted in having both in you. I have always looked up to you and always will, and as annoying as I have been over the years, tagging along and following in your footsteps, you have helped in forming my character.

And finally I want to give a giant thank you to you, my reader. The fact you have taken a chance on this novel and have taken time out of your own life to read it is amazing and it really means the world to me.

About the Author

James E. Rugman was born in Bristol, England on March 16th 1982 and now resides in the Cotswold village of Wotton-Under-Edge with his wife Emily. He is an animal science graduate with a real passion for animal welfare and behaviour. He wrote his debut novel as a hat tip to his studies and as a way of bringing the humble wildebeest to the public's attention. Since graduating from university, James has had a long career in animal welfare before moving into teaching animal husbandry at college level.

Printed in Poland
by Amazon Fulfillment
Poland Sp. z o.o., Wrocław